# D-CITY CHRONICLES

## AJA & RO
## BOOK THREE

## A Novel by
## Annitia L. Jackson

To submit a manuscript for our review, email us at

submissions@majorkeypublishing.com

ROYALTY PRESENTS

MAJOR KEY PUBLISHING

Be sure to LIKE our Major Key Publishing

page on Facebook!

Thank you for taking the time to read my work.

Follow me on my social media to find out about upcoming projects and work:

Website: www.annitialjackson.com

Facebook: https://www.facebook.com/DCityChronicles/?ref=aymt_homepage_panel#

Instagram: https://www.instagram.com/annitialjackson/

Twitter: https://twitter.com/ANNITIALJACKSON

# Acknowledgements

This book is intended to entertain and is recommended for ages eighteen and up. This is a book based on urban fiction which consists of violence, offensive language, and sexual content.

I would like to dedicate this book to my grandmother, Hattie Fletcher. She is my guardian angel in heaven. She taught me to follow my dreams. I will always be indebted to her for that. Love you, Mama!

I just want to take this time to say thanks to my husband, Ron Jackson, for encouraging me and having my back while I took a step out on faith. Thank you for being an amazing father to our son, Nathan, and keeping his five-year-old energy at bay while I wrote. You are my soulmate and helped me to understand what real love is. Thank you for being understanding when I have to write, and you say, "Baby, I got this. You just go do what you need to do." I love you and Nathan to the moon and beyond.

I want to also thank my middle school teacher, Barbara Middlebrooks, for introducing me to writing. You woke up a fire in me that I never knew existed. To my personal reading crew, Zeanola, Undrea, Shawauna, Diedra, Kimessia, and Marcia that would definitely share their opinions both good and bad, I want to thank you for helping me. I love you ladies so much!! I would also like to thank my sister, Kasandra, my cousin, Ingrid, and my nephew, Robert. Also, I would like to thank my aunt Gale for her spiritual guidance. You guys are my inspiration for going after my dream of being an author. I have watched you all accomplish your goals and it inspired me. And to my riders who always have my back, Renee and Freda, I love you both so much.

I also want to thank the ladies in Bookies for taking a chance on my book and helping get the word out about it! Love you, admins!!! Zee, thank you for just being you. You are absolutely amazing and you have been a true blessing to me. Latoya Nicole, you are my inspiration as a mother and an author. You are always so positive and never too busy to offer advice. My Law! I love you to death because you always give me honest and real conversation. You are one of the first people I see in my inbox in the morning, and I know that my mood, if bad, will be lifted. Thank you for reading my work and making me rest LOL.

LIT-erary Plugs!! You ladies are the real MVP's! You ladies are very important to me, and I thank you for reading my work.

I would like to thank God for blessing me with the opportunity to do something that I love to do.

## Prologue- Lily (The Boss)
## (BACK IN THE DAY)

I was on cloud nine! You couldn't tell me anything. I was young, and beautiful, and married to the man of my dreams! I met Calvin at one of my father's parties, and we hit it off. He had just got out of a serious relationship and wasn't looking for anything serious. I knew right then and there I had to have him. He was tall with milk chocolate skin and big eyes. He had a slim, athletic build that looked good with the tailored suit fitted to his body.

I had never been with a Black man before. Hell, I had never been with any man before him. All I knew was that I would do anything to have him. After having him followed, I started planning little accidental meetings that led to flirting and finally dating. Here we were two years later, and I was pregnant with his first child. I was on my way to his office so that I could tell him in person. I had plans for us to go away to our lake house afterwards to make love all weekend and celebrate.

As I was pulling up to the office building, I looked up and saw him pulling out in a red Mustang. It was odd because he had a Cadillac, so I decided to follow him.

I watched as he got out and stopped in front of a rehab center and placed a big, red bow on the car. I wondered if one of his workers was in rehab. I never asked about his drug business, and he never told me. He said it was to protect me in case he was ever arrested.

The mystery was solved when I saw a beautiful Black woman come out that looked vaguely familiar. She came over and hugged him, and he gave her keys to the Mustang. I wasn't stupid. My father had several mistresses growing up, so I knew that infidelity was to be expected of men with power, but something about the way he looked at her rubbed me the wrong way.

I decided to follow them as they pulled off. They had the top down so

I could see them laughing and talking. They weren't touching each other or anything, but I could clearly see a connection between the two of them.

They pulled up to a townhouse that also had a red bow on it. I watched as he came around and opened her door and helped her out. She was excited, and they headed inside. I got out of the car and headed around the back to see if I could peep in the windows and see what I could see. I prayed that my husband wasn't cheating on me and that he was just helping out a friend, but it was just something about the looks he was giving her that let me know my prayers wouldn't be answered.

I saw a small patio and crept up on it and looked in the window. I was in full spy mode and was in search of the truth. My mind was telling me that he was a no good ass dog motherfucker, but something in my heart was trying to convince me otherwise.

I was in the proper position to see everything I needed to see. As I peered through the window, my heart began to slowly crumble. All of my fears were becoming a harsh reality. They were sitting at a table with candles and a whole spread of food. I watched for what seemed like hours of them laughing and talking, but I couldn't hear what they were saying. After a while, I felt stupid because they weren't doing anything but talking, or was I simply telling myself this to ease the pain that snuck its way into my heart. I'd had enough. My heart wasn't prepared to face what was right before my eyes. I was about to leave when I heard something crash. I willed myself not to turn around, but the wife in me, and the spy shit I was on, told me to turn the fuck around and face reality. I looked back in the window, and he was fucking the shit outta her on the kitchen table. The entire spread that was once placed nice and neat on the table, now decorated the floor as if he swiped it away to dive deep into her love tunnel. I felt the hot tears rolling down my cheeks as I looked in his face and saw the love that he had for this woman written all over it. I may sound crazy for saying this, but if it was just sex, I could look past this act of infidelity, but this was something more. My husband wasn't just fucking this woman, he was making love to her. And what hurt most, his face displayed that he had love for her.

I got a better look at her face and realized it was the woman in the locket he kept around his neck. I asked him once before about the locket, and he told me never to touch it. After making love one night, and fucking my husband into a deep sleep, curiosity got the best of me. I was always told that when you go searching for shit, you'd find some shit, and that's when I opened the locket and saw this woman's face. When I saw it, I didn't think she was someone he was fucking. I figured she was dead or something and maybe a relative, but I never thought she was a mistress. *She was a mistress, right? I was his wife.* I thought to myself as I began playing back different scenarios in my head, only to discover that I was a damn idiot for trusting this man.

I looked back at the window and watched him cum in her without a condom. His body began shaking as I watched his ass cheeks get tighter while he pumped with a purpose, making sure his soldiers decorated her pussy walls. I saw the cum oozing and dripping from his rod as he pulled out, and she immediately dropped to her knees, making sure all his sperm was securely inside her body, in one way or another.

It was in that moment that my heart turned to stone. The love I had for Calvin oozed out of my heart like the shit dripping from his cheating dick into this bitch's cum catchers. My stomach cramped up, and I thought about the life I was bringing into this world; the real reason I was trying to make it to his ass in the first place. I wanted to take a brick and toss it through the fucking window, but then I thought, what good would that do? I rubbed my belly and my anger began to grow because he cheated us both. Shit was about to get real bad. Calvin should have learned that not only was I patient, I was calculated.

I felt like I was sleepwalking as I headed back to my car with a bruised heart, but willing myself to not allow this to break me. *I may be bruised, but I'm definitely not broken. Calvin, you fucked over the wrong bitch,* I thought as I slid into my car and made my way home.

Hell hath no fury like a woman scorned. If I didn't believe that before, I certainly believed it now. I drove in silence as my mind began to play out different scenarios and ways for me to get even. I vowed that I would make him and his hoe bitch suffer for breaking my heart and ruining our perfect family. Killing them both would be too easy when I had the option to torture them slowly and take away everything they thought they acquired, bit by bit. I would make their whole family suffer like my father taught me back in the day. I would teach our child to hate him as well. And when the timing was just right, I'd come in like the grim reaper and kill them both. I started thinking of the perfect plan. I pulled into my driveway as a wicked smile stretched across my face. I picked up the phone and dialed the one person I knew who hated my husband more than anything.

"Hello?" he answered after the second ring.

"Doug, we need to meet. I have a business proposition for you. Meet me at Centennial Park in one hour. I am about to make us both rich and take out a common enemy at the same time," I replied.

He chuckled and said, "Anything for your fine ass. See you soon."

That was the beginning of our business together. We became partners in revenge, business, and the bedroom. Calvin, his bitch, and everyone they loved would pay for breaking the heart of Lily Marie Moretti-Simpkins.

## Chapter 1: Aja

I stared at Ace as he delivered the news that Rodney had been killed. I saw the emotions play across my fiancé's face as he took it all in. I was stunned as I watched his eyes get lighter than they ever had before, and I knew Viper was back. Ace had the same expression of worry on his face as I did. A silent look passed between us, and I knew what I needed to do.

I walked over to Viper and wrapped my arms around his body. I nuzzled my nose into the crook of his neck and inhaled the Irish Spring soap he used to shower with earlier. I knew that me being close always seemed to calm him down. I could already hear his heart rate slowing down through his back, and he started stroking my hair. He pulled me in front of him and held me from behind.

"Thanks, baby girl. I needed that. Ace, please tell me that this is all a bad dream. Tell me Raymond didn't kill our father?" Viper asked.

Ace shook his head and said, "Man, Viper, it's true. We need to get to the hospital as soon as possible. We need to move Tyesha, too, before she's next."

Ace went to get Kyra and the car and pulled it around front. I went and took a quick wash up and threw on a black T-shirt dress because I wanted to be comfortable and able to move around. I strapped my knives to my thigh and put on my shoulder holster under the black blazer I put on top. Viper/Ro would be pissed if he knew that I had been training with Kole secretly on self-defense and weapons. At the time, I wanted to be able to protect myself from Romero in case he grabbed me. Now, I wanted to use those skills to protect my family.

We all piled in Ace's Suburban and headed to the hospital. Once we got there, Big Kev met us at the entrance. As soon as Viper got out of the car, he threw a blade hitting Big Kev in the knee. The big man went down hard and grabbed his knee. Viper walked up and yanked the knife out and wiped it on Big Kev's shirt, then said, "The next time I give your ass a job and tell you to stay your ass there, make sure you follow orders! Now get your ass up and go get your shit fixed! I'm letting you live because I know you are loyal and didn't know that Ray was a snake. Next time, your ass will be swimming in my piranha tank. You dig?"

Big Kev nodded, and Viper stepped over him and headed into the hospital.

Ace, Kyra, and I followed behind. I was afraid of what he would do once he saw his father's body. I loved my baby, but he wasn't exactly stable right now, and I was scared of what this was going to do to his condition.

We made it to his father's room and there were police officers and hospital staff standing all around outside the door. One of the policemen had on a brown ill-fitting suit, looked up and started towards us. He asked us to follow him into the private family waiting room, and he closed the door. I was shocked by the next words out of his mouth.

"Ro, man, I got the security tapes before the other detectives could get to them. I gave them to Gunner in the room upstairs. But I brought you in here because a lot has happened in the past hour that you and Ace need to be brought up to speed on."

"I'm sorry, but I'm Aja. And you are?" I asked. I mean, I didn't know who the hell he was, and I wanted to see what I could or couldn't say.

"Sorry, beautiful. I am Detective Mills. I work for Ace and Ro on the force to make sure that they stay off the radar from different investigations. I work homicide, so I am their man on the inside at the department. They pay me well to make things go away," Detective Mills said while winking.

"Mills, cut that winking shit out before you end up flapping an empty eyeball socket. That's all mine right there, and that flirting shit will get you fucked up; put in a leech tank real quick," Viper said without blinking.

Mills nodded that he understood and never made eye contact with me again.

"Look, I need you all to know that we are doing everything we can to resolve everything that has happened within the past hour. I am not sure who you and Ace have problems with, but it looks like they have declared war on the whole D-City Organization. We have people looking all over for the van that…"

"Mills, what the hell does a van have to do with my father being killed, and what do you mean everything? What the fuck is going on?" Viper asked.

I rubbed his hand to calm him down because we wouldn't get any answers if he snapped.

Mills looked confused like he expected us to know what the fuck was going on and said, "I thought Kole would have called you by now. No one has told you about the shit storm that hit about an hour ago?"

Ace jumped up and pulled his gun and aimed it at Mills.

"Stop speaking in circles, and tell us what the fuck is going on," Ace said.

Mills took a breath as Ace sat back down and started telling us what happened.

"Big C was in a car accident. He's in critical condition in the ICU," Mills said.

My heart literally jumped out of my chest. I felt tears running down my face because we just found out about each other, and now, I could lose him.

I felt hands on my face and looked into Viper's light brown eyes.

"Baby girl, please calm down! Big C is strong as fuck, just like his daughter. He will be fine. I promise you," Viper said.

I wiped my face and nodded my head and put it on his shoulder. I was about to ask him to take me downstairs when Kole and Gunner burst through the door out of breath. Kole was covered in blood.

"I've been looking all over for y'all. Mills, did you tell them?" Kole asked.

Detective Mills shook his head no and replied, "No, I just told them about Big C. I was just about to fill them in on the other situation."

Kole looked at Kyra and Ace, and I felt shivers go down my spine because I knew something was terribly wrong.

He bent down in front of Kyra and grabbed her hands. Ace didn't look too happy about it, and I could tell he was about to say something, but Kole interrupted him.

"Ace, it's not like that. I have something I need to tell you both, and I need to look her in the eye when I tell her," Kole said.

Ace stared for a minute and then nodded, letting him know to continue.

Kyra had tears running down her face as if she could sense what was going on.

"Kole, where is my mama and my baby? Why are you covered in blood?"

Kyra asked.

Kole was usually a laidback, easy-going person, but when I looked at his face, all I saw was regret, sorrow, and anger.

He rubbed a hand down his face and told us about leaving the mall and how Aciana was kidnapped. As soon as he said kidnapped, Kyra broke down and fell on the floor, screaming. Ace was pacing the floor with tears in his eyes and

Viper's eyes turned lighter. I felt my own tears running down as I got on the floor and held my best friend as she fell apart

"Kole. Man, did you see who took my baby? Did you recognize them?"

Ace asked.

Gunner and Kole exchanged looks and Gunner said, "Ace, I hacked into the mall security system and downloaded the footage. I didn't want to watch it without you and Viper."

"Yeah, I had him pull the footage because I was too far away to see the license plate or who was in the van. I was too busy trying to get to Aciana and save Ms. Shelly. I promise, Ace, I tried my best to get to them in time, but it was too late," Kole said with a tremble of anger in his voice.

Kyra's head popped up, and she looked straight at Kole.

"Wait. What do you mean you were too late? You should have fucking protected them, Kole!

That's what your damn job is, right? How could you let them be kidnapped!? That's my mama and my baby that you let get taken! We treated you like family and this is the damn thanks we get!" Kyra screamed, bursting into tears again.

Kole's head dropped as he tried to reign in his emotions. I knew how he operated, and I knew he took her words to heart. I could see him blaming himself for them being kidnapped. He looked up into my eyes, and I could tell he was holding something back. I bit the bullet and asked, "Kole, what is it? I can tell there's more. Just go ahead and say it. It can't be worse than my niece being kidnapped."

He looked at Kyra and said, "Ms. Shelly wasn't kidnapped. She was fighting off the kidnappers, trying to stop them from taking Aciana. Unfortunately, they took Aciana anyway. She jumped in front of the van to stop them and they ran her down."

Kyra jumped up and started running out the door. I got up and ran after her along with Ace and Viper. She jumped in the elevator, and we were lucky to catch up with her. We were all silent as we rode downstairs to the emergency room. I watched my best friend, and I had never seen her look like this. I was really worried about her and my nephew growing inside of her.

The door opened, and we ran straight down the hall to the information desk. A blonde haired, blue eyed, male clerk looked up and smiled at us. "Hello, I'm Carl. How can I help you today?"

"My mother was hit by a car, and I need to see if she's okay," Kyra cried.

"Okay, ma'am. What is your mother's name, and I can see about getting someone out to speak to you?" Carl replied.

Kyra gave him her mom's name and he told us to have a seat. Ace and Viper were both on their cell phones barking orders about finding Aciana. I was sitting and rubbing Kyra's back, trying to keep her calm. My babies were doing flips in my stomach, but I dare not say anything or Viper would have me tied to a hospital bed, literally.

About ten minutes later, a nurse came out, calling for the family of Shelly

Williams. We all stood and walked over. She looked at Ace and Viper and gave them hugs. I looked at her and something seemed familiar about her.

"Gentlemen, it seems like I have been giving you bad news all week. The doctor was supposed to come out and speak with you, but unfortunately, he had to go into emergency surgery with an accident victim. Are you related to Shelly Williams?" she asked.

Kyra spoke up and answered. "Yes, I'm her daughter. Is she okay?"

The nurse grabbed Kyra's hand and pulled her into the waiting seat behind us. She rubbed Kyra's back and said, "Baby, your mama was a good friend of mine a long time ago. She was one of the sweetest people I knew. That's how I know that she is with the good Lord now. She is no longer suffering."

Kyra started screaming "MAMA! MAMA! NOOOO! GOD, WHYYYYY!

Kyra lay out on the floor and bawled with tears streaming down her face. She was crying so hard that her chest looked like it was caving in and out.

Ace went over and kneeled down beside her, trying to get her up. She looked at Ace with so much anger, slapped him hard across the face, and started going off.

"This is why I stayed away! You said you would protect us! Get away from me! I hate you! I hate you!" she screamed before collapsing on the floor in a ball and sobbing.

Ace had tears in his eyes but blinked them back up. He bent down and gathered Kyra in his arms and held her closely to his chest.

The nurse looked at him sadly and said, "Young man, can you bring her into the room, please? I need to check her blood pressure, especially since she is pregnant. I am going to page the OB doctor on-call to come and check on her and the baby."

Ace nodded his head and carried a still sobbing Kyra, and we followed the nurse into a room at the end of the hall. Once she was in the bed, her eyes closed, and she drifted to sleep, still crying. Viper, Ace, and I stepped out into the hall once the OB doctor came to check on her.

"Ace, this shit is getting out of hand. Arco is on his way up here with some of the crew so we can head out and find my niece. Motherfuckers think shit is sweet, but they gonna learn today!" Viper growled.

Ace nodded his head in understanding and said, "I just found out about her, man. I can't lose my little girl. Kyra is crushed, man. My baby just lost her daughter and her mama. I'm scared she's going to lose little Ace due to the stress of all this. We need to find out what the fuck is going on ASAP. When I find out who it is, I promise I'm killing everybody in fucking sight. Even the damn goldfish swimming in the motherfucking tank got to die!"

The doctor and the nurse came out the door and let us know that they would be admitting Kyra for a few days because of her blood pressure, and the baby was showing signs of distress. The doctor left and the nurse was about to walk away and I stopped her.

"Excuse me, Nurse? My father was in a car accident and is in the ICU. I was wondering if you could find out which room he is in and someone to give me an update?" I asked.

She smiled and said, "Sure, baby. What's his name and I can find out for you?"

I replied, "It's Calvin Simpkins."

The nurse dropped the charts in her hands and fell to her knees and started bawling. Watching her break down made me want throw my arms around her. I wonder what I said to make her breakdown like this?

## Anise

When she said Calvin's name, my heart literally felt like it left my chest! I really looked at her and she had my eyes. I knew in my heart it was her! I dropped the charts and fell to the floor because my baby that I had lost years ago was standing before me. The tears and pain that had been in my heart for years came pouring out. I was bawling and thanking God for bringing her back to me.

She came towards me and eased down the best she could with her swollen belly. It made me cry harder to know that she was about to become a mother herself. She wrapped her arms around me to comfort me even though she had no clue why I was crying. I was trying to find the words to tell her who I was, but I was afraid of her reaction. Would she hate me? Would we be able to have a relationship after being apart for so long?

"Ma'am, are you alright? Is there anything I can do?" she asked.

I smiled a little because I could see she had a good heart and that made me get up enough courage to tell her. I grabbed her hand and looked at my baby in her beautiful brown eyes and said, "You said that Calvin Simpkins was your father. I have known your father for years. I was once the love of his life. Our love created a beautiful baby girl that was stolen from us. I named her Amara because she brought me so much peace in my life before she was taken."

I had to pause because the emotions were so strong that my voice was trembling, trying to say the words. Tears started falling from her eyes, and when she looked at me, I knew that she knew who I was. She grabbed me and held on so tight, I thought I would burst. We cried together for a few more minutes and then she said, "Your name is Anise, right? You are my real mom?" she asked, with pain and desperation to be loved in her eyes. I could tell my baby had been through hell with just that look.

I knew now wasn't the time for a heart to heart with everything going on, but I wanted to reassure my baby and let her know that she was very much wanted and that I would be here for her. So I replied, "Yes, baby. I am so proud to say that I am your Mama."

She threw her arms around my neck, and I just held on tight. I felt a hand on my shoulder, and it was the young man named Ro trying to get my attention.

"I hate to break this up, but is there somewhere more private that we can all go so you two can talk, and we can have our family meet us at?" he asked.

I stood up and he helped Aja up.

"Yes. Let's go to my office. I am off shift now so we can use it, and no one will bother us," I responded.

Aja grabbed my hand, and we all walked to my office. This was one of the happiest days of my life, and I was thanking God with each step. I had my baby back.

## Chapter 2- Akia

After I found out about my baby girl, I knew who had her instantly. I swear this dumb ass motherfucker had life all fucked up! I promised myself I wouldn't kill anybody until my six weeks maternity leave was up. I looked at the medical staff, and the police, and turned around and walked out of the fucking building because they were wasting my time. I heard them calling my name behind me, but what they failed to realize was that I was in Reaper mode and shit was about to get bad for a lot of people.

"Kia! I know you hear me calling your name!" Tan said, yanking me around.

I actually forgot he was with me because my mind was focused on getting to Rylei and chopping off Ray's balls once I had her.

"Tan, baby, I'm sorry, but I have to find Rylei and those stupid ass cops back there will only get in my way. I know Ray has her, and I don't know what he will do to her. I thought I knew him, but these past few weeks have proven otherwise," I said.

Tan wrapped his arms around me and kissed me on my forehead. I saw him looking in my eyes to see if I was alright, but I was sure he saw no emotions in them. I had shut them off because my baby needed Reaper not Akia. Akia wanted to break down and cry, but Reaper wanted blood. Shutting down was one of the first things that Viper taught me about when I started training.

"I see that look in your eyes, Kia, and believe me, I get it. That's my daughter that he has, too, but we need to come up with a plan to get her back. At least let me call my brother and see if he can pull some video and see who took her out of here," Tan said.

I knew he was right. I had to calm down and not act on impulse. Tan got on the phone and put it on speaker while he held me as we leaned against his car.

Gunner answered in a panicked voice. "Tan, man, I have been trying to reach you for an hour. All hell has broken loose! I thought something had happened to you and Kia. I was just about to turn on the tracking device on your car."

"Gunner, man, some shit went down when we came to see our baby girl.

We think Ray kidnapped her from the clinic. I couldn't answer because we were being questioned by the police. I need you to pull the surveillance tapes and see if it was really him that got my baby girl," Tan replied.

We heard the sounds of typing and Gunner sighed and said, "It will take a minute to download so let me tell you what's been going down over here. Big C was in a car accident and just got out of surgery. He's in the ICU, and they aren't sure if he's going to pull through. Kole was at the mall with Ms. Shelly and Aciana. When they got outside and went their separate ways, a van came out of nowhere and kidnapped Aciana. The worst part is they ran over Ms. Shelly and she died. Kyra and Ace are going crazy over here, man. They put Kyra in the hospital because she and the baby are in danger. She's too stressed out."

I stood there in shock. Not only had somebody kidnapped my baby, but my niece as well. My heart was breaking because Ms. Shelly was a mother figure to us all. Growing up, she would feed us and take us shopping for clothes because April was too drunk or full of dick to give a damn. Now, who would I go to for advice about being a mom?

"Look, we are headed up to the hospital now so we can get a plan together. Have those tapes ready for me when I get there. Since security is fucked here, we might need to move Tyesha and Rodney to our personal safe house. Let Ace and Viper know what's going on," Tan instructed.

"Fuck! Man, that's another thing. Ray came into the hospital and killed Rodney. He tricked Big Kev and came in the hospital and killed his own pops, man. There weren't any cameras in the room so we don't know why he did it. Man, it's some real foul shit going down. Just get here, big brah, so we can handle this shit," Gunner said.

"Alright, Gun. We are on the way." Tan hung up and we stared at each other.

"Kia, it looks like we are at war. Are you ready to deal with this shit and get our daughter and niece back? Because once this is over, we need to sit down and have a talk about your line of work," Tan said as he headed towards the car.

He didn't even give me a chance to respond, so I opened the door and climbed in the passenger's seat. It made me wonder if he was trying to get me to stop contract killing like Ray. I loved Tan, but this was something I loved to do and was good at. I would hate to lose another man, but I wasn't letting anyone tell me what to do either.

We pulled up to the hospital and went to the room that Gunner had texted us to meet him at. We found the room and opened the door to an office. Inside were Ace, Viper, Kole, Gunner, Aja, and an older lady that looked like a nurse. Aja instantly got up and hugged me.

"Kia, I am so sorry about Rylei. I promise we are going to find her and fuck Ray up," Aja said.

Viper jumped up and grabbed her moving her towards the chair and said, "You not doing shit but sitting your pregnant ass down somewhere. Keep on fucking with my seeds and see if I don't fuck your uterus out!"

I saw Aja about to say something back, so I put a stop to it before it got out of hand.

"Gunner, did you get the surveillance tapes downloaded?" I asked.

He pulled out his laptop and turned it on and said, "Yeah, give me a few minutes, and we should be able to view the tapes."

I walked over to the older lady sitting there since no one bothered to introduce us and said, "Hi, my name is Akia but everyone calls me Kia. And you are?"

She stood up and gave me a hug which threw me off, but felt comforting at the same time. I returned the hug and when she let go, she said, "My name is Anise Jones, and I am Aja's real mother. It is so nice to meet you. She has been telling me all about you, and she's right. You are beautiful. I have been praying that they find your little girl soon."

I felt a little of my emotions try and creep back in while in her arms, but I promptly pushed them back down because I couldn't afford to get emotional with everything going on."

"Thank you so much, Ms. Anise. Big C told us about you earlier. I am so happy that you got to be reunited with Aja. She needs a good mother because April wasn't worth shit. Excuse my language, but it's the truth," I replied.

Everybody laughed which lightened the mood for a minute. I sat down in the chair that Tan had brought in for me, and he grabbed my hand and smiled.

I was glad that he was here for me because I needed his strength to keep me from killing everybody in the city. Viper had helped me learn to channel the urges in training.

My phone started ringing, and I looked at the number and saw it was the clinic's number. I knew they were trying to reach me for the police, so I shut it off.

"That reminds me. Let me power my phone back on. I always turn it off when I am on shift," Anise stated.

She powered her phone up and said, "That's strange. I have a message from Calvin. It looks like he might have left it before his accident."

Viper and Ace exchanged looks and got up and stood by the desk.

"Ms. Anise, would you mind putting it on speaker so we can listen to it also?" Ace asked.

She nodded her head yes and put it on speaker as everyone surrounded the desk to listen. The first sound we heard was heavy breathing and a hissing sound.

The next sound we heard was Big C trying to talk through the pain. What he said next had us all in shock.

*"Anise, I don't have long to talk. I don't know if she will come back to finish me off before the ambulance comes. I hope you hear this message in time to save our daughter. I found her, Nise, and she is so beautiful, just like you. Her name is Aja, and she is in danger. My accident was no accident.*

*Lily cut the brake line so I would die, and she could take over my empire. A few minutes ago, my daughter, Camille, came and placed a phone by my ear and Lily said Aja was next. Anise, call Corey and get him here, now! Tell him it's a code twelve, and he will know what to do. Anise, I have always loved you, and if I don't make it, please find our daughter and protect her from that bitch!"*

The phone was silent after that. I guess Big C said what he needed to say or passed out. I looked over at Aja, and I thought I would see tears or fear, but she had coldness in her eyes. It was the same coldness that I saw when I looked at Viper or myself when it was time to kill. My big sis was changing before my eyes.

Viper must have noticed too because he went and stood in front of her and stared at her and said, "Baby girl, I know what you are thinking, and I need you to fall your ass all the way back. Vixen needs to stay back in the past. You are carrying three babies in you, and you need to take care of them. Let us take care of these motherfuckers, and I promise they won't touch a hair on your beautiful head. Plus, we need to plan some shit out, and I know you can help us come up with something to get at them before they get at us."

Aja stared at him for a moment and nodded that she understood. But I wasn't fooled. I knew that look. It was the fake innocent smile that said, "I will pretend to listen, but I am really going to do what the fuck I want to do". I had seen it many times before, but Viper hadn't, and he was being played. I watched him kiss her on the lips and turn around to talk to the fellows. I made eye contact with Aja, and we passed each other a look. We would be doing our own plotting soon.

We smiled at each other, and I looked over and saw Ms. Anise staring at us as if she knew we were up to something.

My thoughts were interrupted by Gunner telling us we could view the footage tapes now. We gathered around to watch the first tape. It was the one from the mall parking area. We saw Aciana and Ms. Shelly going to the car and Aciana sitting on the trunk drinking a juice while Ms. Shelly placed bags in the car.

Out of nowhere, a van pulled up and snatched Aciana and pushed her inside. We watched as Ms. Shelly was fighting the kidnappers, but she was no match for them. She ran in front of the van, and we watched her die right before our eyes. Everyone was silent and emotional for a few minutes seeing what had happened to Ms. Shelly. Kole looked devastated, and I can understand why. Us on the Hit Squad took our jobs seriously, and no matter if we were killing or protecting, we pushed ourselves to be the best. Ace had a tear he quickly wiped away from watching his baby girl taken. He sat up and asked, "I didn't recognize anyone on the tape. Did anyone else? We need to get my baby back as soon as possible. If they can do Ms. Shelly like that, it's no telling what they are doing to her."

I thought about it and something was familiar about the one that grabbed Aciana. I looked at Gunner and said, "Can you play back the part where they grabbed Aciana?"

He nodded and scrolled back the footage. I looked closely and noticed the tattoo on his arm as my own work. I knew the motherfucker that snatched my niece, and his ass was about to die along with his employer.

"I know the one that snatched Aciana. That's Camille's bodyguard, Angelo. He came and got that Italian flag tattoo from me about a month ago."

Ace pulled his cell phone out and started dialing someone.

He put it on speaker and Camille's voice came over the speaker and said, "Hey, baby daddy! Do you miss me already?"

Ace had a look of disgust on his face and said, "Bitch, I know you have my daughter! I don't know what the fuck you and your pale ass mama got going on, but you got life all the way fucked up if you think I will let you get away with taking her!"

Camille started laughing. Ace started pacing, and I knew that he was about to blow the fuck up.

"Aww, sweetheart, I was hoping I had more time with my stepdaughter before you found out. I wanted to bond with her before her baby brother or sister arrived," Camille said.

"Bitch, I just fucked you a few days ago. There's no way you can know you are pregnant. Now, give me my fucking daughter!" Ace yelled.

Camille sighed and responded, "Ace, I am pregnant, and it is definitely by you. When you were looking for Aja and that bitch Kyra you asked me to fly down to relieve your stress as you called it, you got pissy drunk and started calling me that bitch's name and saying how much you loved her. You broke my fucking heart that night, and I knew I was losing you. So, I drugged you the next night, and we fucked three times and you came in me. To ensure that I was pregnant, I also took the two condoms we used right before my flight. I sent them directly to my private doctor who froze them until I could be inseminated. It wasn't needed because I got pregnant from us making love. Our baby will be born in five months."

This bitch really just admitted to basically raping my brother and stealing not only his daughter, but his fucking future kids as well. Before I could say something, Aja had jumped up and grabbed the phone from Ace and yelled, "Your crazy ass better hope I don't find your nasty ass, or I promise you I will skin your ass alive. Now, you have one hour to give me my fucking niece, or I will come looking for your ass. And believe me, Camille, you don't want those problems!"

"Is this my sister-in-law, Aja? Hey, girl! I won't take your threat personally because I understand you are upset and not in your right frame of mind. But, you are pushing my buttons, and believe me, you don't want those type of problems. Now, put my future husband back on the phone so that we can discuss how he can see our daughter. Nice chatting with you! I hope I get an invite to the baby shower, girl. Oh, yeah, and I will tell Romero you said hello." The bitch started laughing.

Aja threw the phone at Ace, sat down, and started rocking and mumbling under her breath. We made eye contact, and we knew no matter what we were going to make that bitch suffer.

"Camille, look, I know you are upset. And believe me, I was foul as fuck for treating you the way I did, but Aciana has nothing to do with this shit. Just give me my daughter, and we can just co-parent our baby once he or she gets here. No hard feelings, no revenge, just two adults working things out. You know I care about you, and this new Camille is not the one that I have been rolling with these past few years. Tell me what I can do to make this right," Ace said.

Camille sighed and said, "There you go trying to play me again. What you fail to realize is that the Camille you knew was an act. I love you, don't get me wrong, but I have always been that bitch. And now, it's time for you to realize it.

I now have control over the empire with my father being out of commission. While you were at the hospital, I raided all your houses and warehouses and retrieved every last brick. Most of your crew is either dead or have taken the raise that I gave them for joining my winning team. Now, as far as what I want, that's easy. You will kill Kyra and marry me. We will be one big happy family, you, Aciana, our baby, and I. I already have our wedding scheduled for two weeks from today. That's enough time for you to mourn and kill that home wrecking bitch. Don't worry, I will let you speak to our daughter every day to remind you of the family waiting on you. Now, I have to go and feed our son. I will call tomorrow and let you speak to Aciana. Bye, my love!"

"Camille? Camille!" Ace screamed into the phone.

Realizing that she hung up, he threw the phone down in frustration.

Ms. Anise came and rubbed Ace's back and said, "Son, you need to calm down and think about the good things you learned from that conversation. Your daughter isn't being mistreated because that crazy bitch wants to be her mother. That means she is probably spoiling her rotten, trying to get her on her side. She wants you and knows that you won't accept her if anything happens to your daughter. Play along with her games until you can figure out a way to find Aciana and get her away from her. Don't lose sight of your goals. Now, I am going to step out in the hall and call my cousin Corey like Calvin wanted me to."

Before she left, Ace asked a question that I had been wondering about.

"Ms. Anise, who is this man named Corey? I heard Calvin and April arguing about him."

She smiled and said, "Corey is the source that you get your supply from.

I know you are wondering how I know this. It's because he is my cousin and lives in Cuba. He and his brother run the cartel there. Corey had to leave the states because he's wanted by the FBI, thanks to April snitching, but that's another story for another time." She left out, typing on her phone.

Gunner cleared his throat and started talking. "I have the footage from the clinic up and running when you are ready, Tan and Kia."

I looked at Tan, and he grabbed my hand and squeezed it. I knew that this was going to be hard to watch. Someone taking my baby girl out of a place that I thought was safe for her. I still owed Doc a kick to the balls when I saw him next. He better be glad that he wasn't there at the time.

Gunner brought the laptop over, and we watched it for a few minutes until we saw the nurse that we paid to watch over her take her from her crib and hand her over to that nasty bitch that Ray was fucking. Now, mind you, this bitch was crying and screaming when I left the clinic that she wasn't the one that handed my daughter over to that skank. Not only were Ray and the skank going to die, the nurse was going to suffer as well.

"Gunner, did the police see the tape yet?" Tan asked.

Gunner shook his head no and replied, "Naw, brah. They were going through the footage but hadn't reached that part yet. I sent a virus through to corrupt the files so they can't retrieve it. I also got the address for the nurse that handed over my niece. Looking through her financials, her dumb ass deposited five thousand dollars an hour ago. I already hacked her accounts and sent the money into the account I set up for Rylei. Make sure y'all make that bitch suffer when you go to her house."

"You already know, Gunner. This bitch will pay for fucking giving my baby over to that bitch. Tan, we need to head over to the warehouse to retrieve some items that I will need. I also need to change into something more comfortable than this maxi dress," I responded.

"Ace and Viper, are you coming?" Tan asked.

Ace and Viper both nodded their heads yes. Then Viper started leaving instructions for Kole, Gunner, and Aja.

"Kole, take Aja to Tan's safe house. Ray doesn't know about that one. I need you to guard her with your life, literally. If anything happens to her, Kole, I promise you Zontae will have to scrape your skin off the floor. Don't let her talk you into doing some shit that will get you fucked up. Gunner, I am sending you to the cabin with Doc and Tyesha. This hospital ain't worth shit with security, and I need for you to protect her. She could have information once she wakes up. Big C will be joining as soon as he is stable enough to travel. His damn wife and fruit loop ass daughter could have someone finish the job," Viper said.

Aja spoke up and said, "Ace, I think you should send Kyra down there as well. She's not in the right frame of mind to be going through this shit.

I am worried about her and your unborn son. At least Doc can watch her there and make sure she is okay."

"Yeah sis, you're right. We will send her with them. I have no clue what Camille is capable of, especially since she wants her dead. I have to figure out a way to outsmart that bitch and her damn mama. Her family is in the mob, so I am sure they are getting help from them. We need more fire power to help take down these motherfuckers for good."

We all nodded our heads. We knew we were definitely outnumbered thanks to Camille killing off a chunk of them and bribing the rest of them to switch sides.

None of us saw Ms. Anise come in, but she must have heard him say we needed help because she said, "You are about to get all the help you need. Corey and his brother are headed here now.

They are on their private jet now. They are bringing their soldiers with them."

"I thought that Corey was wanted by the FBI? Why is he risking his freedom coming to help us with this mess?" Aja asked.

Ms. Anise looked nervous and then took a deep breath and said, "Big C and him were friends for many years. Any beef that Calvin has, Corey has. He knows that Calvin's daughter is in danger, and Aja is his goddaughter so he is stepping up and coming to protect her. But the main reason is because his granddaughter has been kidnapped."

"What do you mean his granddaughter? Who is she?" I asked.

"Aciana is his granddaughter. Corey is Ace's father," she answered.

I thought, *"Well, damn! Leave it to April to fuck another man of power."*

## Chapter 3-Gena

I watched my man pace the floor with Rylei in his arms. He had been cussing me out for the past hour, but I didn't give a damn. He said he wanted his daughter, and I got her for him. It only cost him five thousand dollars so he should be happy. To me, he was acting like a bitch, being scared of his ex-fiancée. I mean, this nigga was really shook like she was going to come through the door like Michael Myers or some shit!

That bitch couldn't hold a candle to me on my worst day. I was the definition of what a real woman should be. I cooked for my man, cleaned, and fucked him into a coma any time he wanted this good ass pussy. Kia was too damn strong of a Black woman for a man like him. I knew his likes, wants, and desires. I should because I had been studying his ass for damn near four months.

I only worked at that chicken restaurant because it was his favorite place to eat, and I knew

I would run into him eventually. It was my job to keep him happy and under control. I was getting paid well to do so. I knew I had to do damage control so let the kissing ass begin.

"Baby, I am so sorry! I only wanted you to have her because you said she would be better off with us. You know I just want to make you happy. Please don't be mad at me!" I cried, making sure the fake tears fell down my face.

I watched his face soften, and I knew I had him. I was smiling on the inside.

He placed Rylei in her crib and kneeled down in front of me. He wiped the tears from my face and stared at me with so much love. I would be moved if I had any emotions, but I didn't, so he was shit out of luck.

"Gena, baby, I am so sorry. I know you only did this for me, and I am grateful.

I just wished you would have told me what you were doing beforehand. Now we have to be more careful because Kia is going to be out for blood, literally! I don't want you hurt because you were trying to do something for me. You're my wife, and it's my job to protect you," Ray said.

Yes, we are married. A few days ago, we went to Vegas, and I talked him into getting married. Being Mrs. Raymond Casey would go a long way in our plans. I smiled down at this dumbass fool as he had tears in his eyes. I am sure he thought it was a loving smile, but really, I was trying not to laugh.

"I know, baby. And I love being your wife. I feel safe with you and know you would die for us. I know how you feel about leading, and I should have waited on you to lead us, baby. I promise not to do it again. At least, we have our daughter now and our family is complete," I responded.

Ray smiled and kissed me on the lips passionately. If it was my boo, I would have been turned on. But unfortunately, it was his non-stroking ass. He had the equipment but damn sure didn't know how to use it. I was surprised Kia even got pregnant. I mentally threw up in my mouth from him touching me. I just was not in the mood to fake another orgasm. I gently pushed him away and said, "Ray, baby, since you made me ruin dinner, can you go and pick us up some dinner at Zaxby's? You know how much I love their salads. Plus, I am still a little sore from our honeymoon."

He laughed and responded, "Daddy put it down, didn't he?"

I wanted to tell him it was sore from him pounding away with his no stroke having ass, but that would blow my cover. So, I just laughed and nodded my head yes. He kissed me on my forehead and then kissed Rylei before leaving out to grab the food. I watched from the window as his truck pulled out of the driveway. As soon as he was gone, I pulled out my burner phone and called my father. He picked up on the third ring.

"Gena, I heard you have Kia's baby and you married Ray. Good job, baby girl. Now, you just need to get him to put you on all his accounts so we can clean his ass out. Rodney never had a chance to change his will, so Ray and Ro should inherit all his money and assets. Ro should be taken care of soon. Then, baby girl, we can get rid of Ray, and you will be one rich widow," Dad said.

I smiled, thinking about all the money that I stood to gain. My bae was already paid, but hell, you can never have enough money. I was ready to get out of the country, travel, and spend my millions. We had plans to escape together and be the happy couple we were meant to be.

"Baby girl, I have to go. We need to meet soon so we can go over everything. Just make sure to keep him happy so we can keep him in control. Keep an eye on the baby, too. Once they are all dead, we can sell her for a lot of money. I already have a few couples in mind. We will talk soon, and

71

don't forget to get him to sign those papers," my dad said.

I replied, "I understand, Dad. Just make sure that you hurry up and kill them.

I am ready to get the hell away from here and live my life. I will take care of everything on my end, and you do the same."

I pushed the end button because I heard Ray coming up the stairs. My father and I didn't do the whole I love you crap anyway. We just had a mutual understanding that we would use each other's skills to get rich. I was down with that because I only had emotions for one person, and my father was not that person. I knew that later tonight I would have to put on another performance and fake an orgasm with the dry sex to come. I couldn't wait for Ray to die.

## Romero

I was smiling from ear to ear knowing that my brother was dead. Now, I just needed Ro to die, and my life would be complete. Doug, Derrick, and I were in the warehouse with all the drugs we had stolen from the D-City Boyz.

We had killed most of their crew and bribed the ones that were left. I couldn't wait to get home and make love to my angel. She was the most beautiful pregnant woman I had ever seen.

"Romero, did you hear what I said? Lily said that Camille was on her way to tell us the plan for dealing with Ro and his crew. I can't wait for them to get what they deserve. My family was supposed to rule this city any fucking way, but Big Roland stole it from my father," Doug said.

I don't know why he kept saying that shit. Hell, I hated my father and killed his ass for that very reason. But he wasn't a thief. Doug's father was simply jealous of what my pops had. Pops wasn't letting Doug's dad into the organization because he was a fuck up. The only thing he was good at was pimping pussy and selling babies. I didn't want to start shit because I still needed his ass, so I said, "Yeah, Pops shouldn't have done that shit. Hey, do you really think Lily is retiring for good? I mean, I have met her daughter, but she is kind of young to lead. I don't know why she didn't put one of us in charge. It would have made more sense. I hear she's hung up on Ace. What if that motherfucker makes her change her mind and say fuck us? We need to keep an eye on her to make sure everything is on the up and up," I stated.

Doug nodded his head and we continued overseeing the distribution to the new trap houses we had set up around the city. Camille called and said we had to put off the plan for another week, so we finished everything up and headed out of the building. After chatting for a few, we headed our separate ways.

I was headed back to my townhouse in Murfreesboro. My baby and I had moved in after Rodney was killed. I decided that I would fix her a candle light dinner with some barbecue pork chops and loaded mashed potatoes. She loved mashed potatoes since she had become pregnant.

I pulled over into Publix and headed into the store. As I was pushing my cart, I looked down the aisle and saw someone that looked just like my Aja.

As I got closer, I realized it was her. I wondered what she was doing at the store without telling me. I walked up behind her and rubbed her hair as she turned around. She had a look of shock on her face. I guess she wasn't expecting to see me here.

"Angel, what are you doing out this time of night with my baby boy? Why didn't you call me? I would have picked up whatever you were craving and brought it home for you," I said.

She continued to stare at me for a moment and shook her head as if she was clearing it. She rolled her eyes at me and replied, "Yeah, I was craving some mac and cheese, and I didn't have the supplies to make it at home. Now, I think I just want to go home. I'm not feeling well all of a sudden."

My heart leapt in my chest. I hope nothing is wrong with my seed. I know she lost our first child, and I didn't want her to lose this one. So, I asked her if she needed to go to the hospital, and she shook her head no, but said she needed to go to the restroom. I told her go ahead, and I would be waiting up front so I could pay for our groceries. After heading to the registers and paying for our food, Aja came back and we walked out into the parking lot. I opened the door for her and buckled her in and placed a kiss on her cheek. I went to the trunk to put the groceries in so we could get home since it was so late. Hardly anyone was out, but you could never be too careful. I bent down to move some bags over and I felt a sharp pain in the back of my head. Before I knew it, darkness closed in and I was out.

# Chapter 4- Aja

I was a little upset that I couldn't be out with everyone else looking for my niece. I stayed at the hospital for a while and helped Gunner and Kole plan out the move for Kyra, Tyesha, and Calvin. We talked Anise into going with them to the cabin to be extra medical support for Doc and his team. Calvin was stable enough to be moved, but would need round the clock care. Doc went down to Gatlinburg earlier and was changing the downstairs basement into a mini hospital for our loved ones.

Anise said she wanted to talk to me about everything, but too much was going on right now, and we agreed to get to know each other better once everything had settled down. She told me that Tyesha was my sister which shocked the hell out of me. Tyesha definitely wasn't my favorite person, but she had been through a lot, so I wanted to make sure she was at least safe. Plus, she was my sister, and I at least wanted to attempt to have a relationship with her and my nieces.

Once we saw everyone off in the ambulances Anise had ordered, we headed to Tan's safe house out in Murfreesboro. Tan had told us that there was no food so we stopped at the Publix down the street to pick up some groceries. I was tired, ready to eat, and lay down, so I told Kole what I needed on the next aisle so we could get the shopping done faster.

I felt something brush my hair and turned around. Standing before me was my worst nightmare. Romero was staring at me and talking as if we were a happy couple. I always knew he was sick, but now I knew for sure this motherfucker was delusional. I decided to play along so I could get away from him and get some help. He told me he would be up front since I had to go to the bathroom. As soon as he started pushing his cart off, I flew down the aisle to find

Kole. I found him two aisles over as I kept looking behind me to make sure Romero wasn't following me.

I grabbed Kole and said, "Romero is here! His delusional ass thinks we are a couple, and I am going home with him. We have to get his ass now so we can kill him. There is no way in hell I want him alive when my kids are born."

Kole stood there shocked before pulling out his phone and dialing rapidly. I heard Ro's voice instantly come through the speakers and say, "Kole, what's up? How's my baby?"

I smiled because he was always thinking about me. I could tell by the calm timber in his voice that it was Ro. Viper's tone was always rougher.

"Man, some crazy shit just happened at the store. Aja was shopping, and Romero walked up to her talking as if they were a couple. I think his ass has snapped or some shit. Aja thinks we can grab him, but I had to call you first to see how you wanted me to handle it," Kole explained.

"Is he near her now? Kole, you want to get fucked up! Get her the fuck away from there now! It's only you two, and it could be a setup. There could be a whole crew of motherfuckers waiting to grab your asses as soon as you get in the parking lot. Find an exit and get her out of there. Send the location to my phone and get Aja to the safe house. We will meet you all there in twenty minutes. Protect my babies, Kole, or I promise I will forget you are family," Ro said.

The line went silent so Kole put his phone back in his pocket and said, "Aja, I am going to look around the back of the store for an exit and to see if the coast is clear. Go over there to the women's bathroom and wait in there until I come and get you."

I nodded and headed slowly towards the bathroom. I watched as Kole disappeared down the hallway. As soon as he was out of sight, I made a beeline towards the front of the store. Fuck it! I was tired of running and hiding from his sick ass! This was the best time for us to get him, and I was going to do it no matter the costs. I checked my purse and my Taser X26C was snug in the side pocket. I walked to the registers and started smiling at Romero. I watched his eyes light up like I was the most beautiful thing he had ever seen. Shit, I was smiling because I was about to fuck up his world.

We got out to his car and he buckled me in like I was a little child and placed a kiss on my cheek. I instantly felt sick to my stomach, and my babies were kicking the hell out of my kidneys, but Mama had plans, and they needed to calm their little asses down. He didn't shut the door, so it made it easier for me to get out and around the side of the car.

I looked around to make sure no one was watching. It was almost 2:00 a.m. and there were only two cars parked in our section, Romero's and Kole's. I had my Taser in my hand and took the safety off. I watched as he bent down into the trunk and I fired at the back of his head watching the barbs go in. His body hit the ground and started shaking like he was having a seizure. His eyes were rolling in the back of his head and he was foaming at the mouth. I swear I had a damn orgasm watching his sick ass suffer. I heard footsteps and started to pull the gun from my back when I saw that it was Kole.

"Aja, what the fuck! Man, why the fuck did you leave the fucking bathroom! Are you trying to get me killed? Man, Ro is going to have a damn fit about this shit! Get in the fucking car while I get his big ass in the trunk!" Kole yelled, grabbing Romero and dragging him towards the trunk of the car.

I unlocked the car with the keys he had tossed me and sat down and buckled up. Now that I had time to think, I realized that I was in some deep ass trouble. My damn psycho ass fiancée was going to whoop my ass when he found out what I just did. I shook my head and said a prayer because all hell was about to break loose.

# Ro

I had Kia hauling ass down the interstate so we could get to Aja. Luckily, it was late at night and there wasn't much traffic out, but it still took us 45 minutes instead of the 20 minutes I wanted it to be. I kept picturing in my mind Romero killing Kole and taking my baby away from me. Earlier, I came back and was in the car with Tan, Kia, and Ace. They filled me in on everything that happened at the hospital and we started searching for information on where to find Aciana and Rylei. It was hard because most of our crew had been killed or switched sides. We had a few leads, but nothing concrete.

My phone rang, and it was Kole. I put it on speaker because I figured that Aja was giving him trouble about not being able to search for the girls. I was pissed the fuck off when he told me that Romero was near my baby. I was worried that Viper would make an appearance, but surprisingly, I was still here, scared to death, and worried about my family.

We pulled up to the safe house, and I jumped out, running to the door. Everyone else jumped out and followed behind me. I entered in the code and headed up the stairs. I stopped when I heard a man screaming. All of us took our guns out and crept down the hall towards the living area. When I peeped around the corner, I saw Aja cooking in the kitchen and Kole sitting at the table reading the paper. The screams from the spare bedroom were getting louder. It was a good thing that this area was secluded and had no neighbors.

I signaled for everyone to put their guns down and headed around the corner. Kole was the first one to see me, and as dark as he was, he turned pale. I knew then that some shit had gone down that I wouldn't like.

"Hey, Ro. Man, I promise you I followed your orders, but her ass is just as crazy and stubborn as you." He started to say more but Aja interrupted him.

She wrapped her arms around my neck and kissed me with so much passion, my dick automatically stood at attention. When she finished, she smiled and stared deeply in my eyes. I promise I almost forgot where the fuck I was at and what I was doing until I heard the screams coming from the other room again.

"Who the fuck is in the back room screaming Aja?" I asked.

I watched her face and her smile faltered a bit, but she recovered quickly and said, "Big Kev is back there right now. He needed to let off some steam. I fixed you some of your favorite foods, baby. I have country fried steak, mashed potatoes, and corn on the cob. I know you all have to be hungry after the day you've had. Did you find out anything about the girls?"

I looked at her and then looked back at Kole who put his head down. Okay, her ass was trying to stall and shit. That's alright. I had something for her ass since she wanted to be slick.

"Sis, you cooked? Hell yes. I'm hungry. Let's eat. Come on Ace and Tan before I eat all this shit up and you won't have a damn thing but crumbs," Kia said, walking over to the table.

Her ass thought she was slick too. I saw that look they gave each other. Kia was trying to help Aja by changing the subject. Ace and Tan went to the table and Aja started fixing plates. As soon as she turned towards the stove, I headed towards the bedroom door. I was about to open the door when I heard her yell stop, but she wasn't stopping shit. Her ass was hiding shit from me and that was about to stop. I opened the door and the sight before me had me heated. Big Kev had Romero chained to the ceiling with his hands above his head and his feet spread apart chained to the floor.

He had a bat wrapped in barbed wire and he was hitting Romero repeatedly in the area where his dick was laying, or should I say part of his dick. There were chunks missing and one of his balls was gone.

The floor was a bloody mess with chunks and shit everywhere. Big Kev stopped and nodded his head acknowledging me. He picked up a blowtorch and sealed off Romero's wounds. Romero passed out as soon as skin started charring. I turned around and pulled the door closed behind me. Somebody was about to give me some fucking answers!

I walked over to Kole and just stared. He cleared his throat and proceeded to tell me how Romero ended up here and Aja's part in it. I looked over at her with a deadly look, and her ass took off running and slammed the master bedroom door. I heard the locks click, letting me know she had locked herself in. Like that shit was going to stop me.

"Ro, I know you are pissed, but that's still my sister. And you can't put your hands on her. Why don't you sit down and eat and try to calm down before you talk to her? That way, you can go in with a clear mind and not be so angry when you talk to her. Remember, she is pregnant, and we as women go through so many emotions during that time. I bet she didn't even think about what she was doing. It was probably just her hormones," Kia explained.

I stared at her because she really thought I was listening to her ass. Ace and Tan looked at me and I nodded at them. Ace said, "Handle your business, brah. She knew better than to do that shit!"

Kia was about to say something when Tan scooped her ass up and carried her up the stairs. I went to the kitchen drawer and got zip ties, putting them in my pocket. I walked down to the locked door and kicked that motherfucker straight in, splitting the door frame. She screamed and ran towards the bathroom. I caught her ass and picked her up before she could close the door. I dumped her on the bed and zip tied each one of her hands to the headboard. I moved down and did the same thing to her ankles. I made sure her legs were spread wide. I looked up and she had tears running down her face, and I almost stopped my plans. But when I saw my babies moving in her belly, I knew she needed to be taught a lesson. I tore the dress off of her as well as her panties and sports bra. I stared down at her and left the room. I wanted her ass to think about what I was going to do to her.

I closed what was left of the door behind me and went to the kitchen and fixed myself a plate. I sat down to eat as Ace and Kole stared at me, probably wondering what I did to Aja. But fuck that. She was my fiancée, and I could do whatever the fuck I wanted to. I finished my plate and washed the dishes. I told Ace goodnight and told Kole he was on first shift for guard duty tonight. Then I punched his ass right in the eye and said, "Next time she gets away from you and puts herself in danger, I promise you they won't be able to identify your body without dental records."

I walked off and headed into the bedroom. I saw her watching me from the bed with tears in her eyes. I wanted to choke her ass or bend her over my knees and whoop her ass, but she was carrying my babies, and I couldn't chance hurting them. So, I had another form of torture waiting on her.

Going over to the dresser, I grabbed a bed sheet out and grabbed the duct tape out of my pocket. I heard her inhale a breath and knew she was wondering what I was going to do. I ain't gonna lie, my dick was hard thinking about my plans for her. I walked over to the door and used the tape to tape the sheet over the broken door so no one could see in.

I walked over to the bed and started taking off my clothes. When I was fully naked, I joined her on the bed and whispered in her ear.

"What you did tonight could have cost you not only your life, but the life of our children. The only thing saving you now is the fact that you are carrying my seeds. You tied to this bed because your ass doesn't listen. I am going to make you suffer for putting my seeds at risk. I want you to remember this night every time you think about putting your life or my kids' lives at risk."

I trailed my hand down her body, using my fingers to lightly brush against her skin. I circled her nipple first, knowing they were sensitive and saw goose bumps form on her skin. I placed my tongue on the outer part of her nipple and licked a circle around them. I heard her moan, and knew I was on the right track. I eased my hand down her

93

stomach and down the top of her pretty ass bare pussy. I looked down and already saw the juices glistening on her pink lips. I used my fingers to trace an outline around her outer lips and moved closer to her clit. I kept circling, getting closer and closer, but never touching. She was moaning and thrashing around against her bound hands.

I licked my way down her body and started licking all the juices that were running from her body. No matter how much I licked up, it just kept coming. I slowly moved my finger to her opening and eased in my finger. I started moving it in and out slowly, making sure to do a come here motion to hit the spot that she loved the most. I inserted another finger in and started moving faster.

"Shit. Ro, baby, that feels so good," Aja moaned.

I smiled to myself because I wanted her to feel like she was about to explode. I pulled my hand out and she whined. I replaced my fingers with my tongue and started sucking on her clit. My hand was still slick with her juices, and I moved it over my dick and started using the juices to start stroking my dick that was brick hard. I knew it wouldn't be long until I exploded because watching her sex faces and hearing her moan was driving me crazy.

I stuck my tongue in her pussy and started fucking her with it like it was my dick. I felt her walls clenching it and felt myself getting harder.

"Oh, shit. Baby, I'm about to cum!" she moaned.

I immediately stopped and pulled my tongue out.

"Why did you do that? I was cumming!" she cried.

I was still stroking my dick and could tell I wasn't far from nutting, and I needed her to pull it out of me so I said, "Shut up and catch this nut real quick."

I didn't give her a chance to adjust. I just started fucking her mouth as she wrapped her lips around it and suctioned her jaws. Spit was running out and I grabbed a pillow and put it under her head so she wouldn't choke. As soon as she was propped up, I started hitting her tonsils, making her gag. My baby was a pro though. She adjusted and started making my toes curl. I moved my hand and started rubbing her button getting her wet all over again.

I felt myself about to explode, and I pulled out and nutted all over her beautiful breasts. I then moved down her body and rubbed the tip of my dick on her clit with the rest of the seeds that was oozing from it. I heard her moan and knew she was about to cum. I stopped and got up to go in the bathroom. Before I could go in she yelled, "Ro, you not going to finish me off!"

I went back and looked her in the eye and said, "Hell naw! Women who listen and don't put themselves in danger get to cum and get this dick. Women that don't listen have to suffer and be without dick for two days. Now think about that with your pregnant, horny ass."

I went in the bathroom and slammed the door. There were more ways to get my point across than pain. Next time she thought about risking her life, I hoped she would think back on this shit. Aja was freakier than I was and holding out on giving her this dick was punishment enough.

## Chapter 5- Ace

I couldn't sleep last night because all I could think about was my baby girl and what Camille could be doing to her. I mean, I didn't think she would hurt her since she said she wanted to be her mom, but the bitch was crazy and that thought alone gave me pause. I couldn't believe she had fooled my ass all these years, making me think she was normal and a good girl. Her ass had been plotting against us all, and I never saw it coming. That bitch had played me like a fucking fiddle. I looked at the clock and saw it was 4:00 a.m., so I decided to get out of bed and go sit on the patio and blow one.

Everyone was asleep, except Big Kev, who took over watch from Kole a few hours ago. I gave him a head nod as he drank coffee and watched the screens and headed off to the patio. I opened the sliding doors and stepped out into the hot, muggy air. The sun wasn't up yet so the lights around the pool were illuminating the large backyard. I pulled out my smoke and lit it, inhaling and taking in my scenery. I was trying to clear my mind and think of ways to get out of the situation I was in and get my daughter back, but nothing was coming to mind. I usually talked to Aja about my problems, but I knew that was a no-go because her ass was on lockdown. I pulled out my phone and dialed Kyra, praying she was awake.

"Hello?" she answered in a sad tone.

I felt so bad for my baby. Not only had she lost her mom, but our daughter was kidnapped, too. Add that to the fact that she was pregnant and stressed out.

"Hey beautiful, I didn't wake you, did I?" I asked.

She sighed and replied, "No, I couldn't sleep. Junior has been sitting on my bladder, and I have been in the bathroom more than the bed. Doc gave me something to relax a little, so I have just been trying to rest. I'm sorry about blowing up earlier. When Kole wakes up, I need to apologize to him, too. I shouldn't have blamed him for everything that happened. I know how much he loves Aciana."

"I'm sorry, Ky. This shit is all my fault. If I hadn't been fucking with her crazy ass, none of this would have happened. Your moms would be alive, and Aciana would be safe in her bed. I swear to you, Ky, I'm going to get our baby back and make this shit up to you," I said.

I felt like shit for not being able to keep my family safe. I was mad that Kyra kept my daughter away from me to keep her safe. Now, I see what my lifestyle was doing to my family. This shit wasn't worth it, and as soon as this nightmare ended, I was taking my family and getting the fuck out of Nashville.

"Ace, I don't blame you for this shit, either. No one knew that damn girl was crazy. Gunner told me everything that she said at the hospital. I'm just upset with myself that I'm not strong enough to be there for you right now. My mama's death is hitting me really hard, and the only thing keeping me halfway sane right now is the child that I am carrying in my stomach. After Doc told me I was risking his life, I have been trying to calm down because I don't want to lose him," she said, with a sniffle.

I replied, "Ky, baby, don't cry. You won't lose my son. He's strong like his pops. Just take it easy and let me worry about getting our daughter back. I wish I could take away the pain of you losing your moms. I would do anything to bring her back to you. I promise that when I get our daughter back we will leave Nashville for good and raise our family. I can't keep putting you all in danger. I love you and my kids too much for that shit. I've got more than enough money to take care of us. The only thing I need for you to do is keep my seed safe inside you and pick where you want us to live. Can you do that for me baby?"

She giggled and answered, "Yeah, I can do that for you. Are you sure you are ready to leave the game behind? You know that I would never ask that of you. I know how much you love being in charge, and I have seen the rush you get when you make a deal. I just don't want you regret giving it up later on and resent me for it. Hustling is in your blood, and I think you would get bored not having anything to replace that rush. Plus, what about Kia and Aja? You know how you are about your sisters, and you mean to tell me you would leave them here? Ace, I love that you want to change your life to keep us safe, but I also want you to be happy."

I smiled because I truly realized how much of a good woman that Kyra was, just by her thinking about what would make me happy. She could've said, "Hell yeah, let's leave everybody behind and think about ourselves", but my baby was thinking about my happiness. She just didn't know it, but I had plans for her as soon as this shit was over. I was tired of being away from her and my babies.

"Alright I hear you, shorty. Let me think on some things, and we can talk later about the future. Now, I need you to lie down and get some sleep so my son can meet his pops in about four months. Can you do that for me baby?" I asked.

She giggled and replied, "Yes, daddy. I can do that for you. I just need you to do a couple of things for me since I am away. Ask Aja to make the funeral plans for my mama. Aja was like a daughter to her, so she will know what to do. I also need you to be safe, Ace. I don't know what I would do if I lost you, too. So, I need for you to bring our daughter and yourself back safely to me."

I smiled and said, "I gotcha, shorty. Is there anything else that you need before I hang up?"

There was a pause, and I thought that maybe we got disconnected until I heard her say, "Make sure that bitch suffers before you kill her!"

"You have my word, shorty. I love you, Ky."

"I love you too, Ace."

I pushed the button to end the call and sat and thought about what I could do to make this all end. I had a thought and decided to see where it took me. I sent a text on my phone for Camille to call me. Not more than five minutes later, my phone was ringing. I answered and said, "What's up, Camille? How are my daughter and our baby doing?"

She started chuckling. "Really Ace, I know you don't give a fuck about our baby. Who are you trying to fool? Now, is that bitch dead yet? That is the only thing I want to talk about. Our daughter is asleep in her new princess themed bedroom. Nothing is too good for my daughter."

I really wanted to choke the hell out of this bitch, but I had to play along.

"Can I just see her to make sure she's okay? I mean, we can FaceTime, and that way, I can make sure she's safe. Can you at least do that for me?" I asked.

Two minutes later, her crazy ass face popped up on my screen. She had the nerve to be smiling like shit was sweet between us. I remember at one time her beautiful face would make me smile. Now, I wanted to take a knife and carve her fucking face off.

"See, I can be agreeable when you ask nicely. Now, let me turn the camera around so you can see our daughter," she said, smiling.

The room was huge and decorated in pink, mint, and a cream colors. It had all her favorite princesses on the wall and a ton of toys everywhere. There were pictures on the wall of Camille and I that had been taken over the years.

She moved over to a big, pink and gold, round, canopy bed that held my princess.

She was asleep with her mouth open, sprawled out across the bed. She had on a pink, silk pajama set, and I was happy I didn't see any marks on her.

Camille backed out of the room and closed the door. Wherever they were, the house was big. She went into what I assumed was her bedroom and said,

"Well, you have now seen that our daughter is safe and happy. Now, you need to make her mommy happy and marry me. I would hate to have to tell our baby that her father and mother died. Then, I would have to sell her to the highest bidder because I wouldn't be able to look at her without thinking about you. So, my love, what's it going to be?"

I ran a hand down my face because I was stuck between a rock and a hard place. I had to go along with this shit long enough to get my daughter back and kill that bitch and her mama. This shit literally had me sick to my stomach.

"Yeah alright, I will marry you. But, I am not waiting to do this shit in two weeks. We can go down to the courthouse in the morning and get that shit over with. Then, I want my daughter back afterwards," I replied.

She smiled in the camera like I had actually proposed to her ass.

"Baby, I am so happy you want to marry me. But, I am not a fool so don't try and treat me as such. I am a boss bitch, and I run this city. And soon, I will run you. I will agree to marry you tomorrow, but not at the courthouse. We can do it at the little wedding chapel that sits on State Street. Then, you will move in with me in two weeks. That will give that bitch two weeks to mourn her mama, and then she will be joining her in the afterlife. And you will be the one to pull the trigger. Do I make myself clear, husband?" she asked.

"Yeah, I get it. Just make sure no one lays hands on my daughter," I reluctantly responded.

She laughed and said, "Good. Meet me at the chapel at 11 a.m. sharp.

I expect you to have a flawless diamond ring for me, at least ten carats in a platinum setting. Make sure to wear a suit, and tell Ro to be on his best behavior. I would hate to get my wedding dress bloody because your best man got on my bad side. Tell your sisters to wear red. They will be my bridesmaids since we will be family soon. Our son is making me hungry, and I have a lot to do before tomorrow morning. Make sure to get some rest for our wedding night. I expect that tongue to be on point. Enjoy your last day as a single man, my love."

The screen went blank and I lowered my head in my hands.

"Please tell me you really aren't about to give in and marry that bitch!" Kia said.

I damn near pissed on myself. I didn't even hear her ass open the door.

I looked at her, and it appeared by her attire that she had been working out or running.

"What the fuck Kia! Why you sneaking up and shit on your brother? I could have had my gun and shot your ass!" I screamed.

Kia started laughing like I was cracking Kevin Hart jokes or some shit and replied, "Boy, please! First of all, you don't have your gun on you. Your pockets are the same size, and there are no bulges under your shirt. Second, I would have killed you by now if I wanted you dead. I have been standing here for ten minutes. You forget what I do for a living, big brother. Now, please tell me you have some type of plan to kill that bitch before she becomes my sister-in-law. A bitch looks good in red, but I would love for that red to be her blood."

I looked at my sister, and her ass was dead serious. I had never seen this side of Akia. And to be honest with you, that shit was scaring me a little bit. Her eyes were colder, and her voice took on a serious tone when she talked about Camille's blood. When this shit was over, we were going to sit down and have a serious talk about her chosen profession. I didn't want my little sister getting like Viper and shit. I basically raised her, and I would be damned if I let her sell her soul.

"Kia, do you hear how you sound right now? When the fuck did killing become your career goal?" I asked.

She shrugged her shoulders and said, "It's something that I am good at, and I like to do it. Nothing traumatic happened to me or no shit like that. I just like the thrill I get completing a mission. It's just like you get a thrill from being a kingpin.

Now, I will ask you again. What are we doing about that bitch?"

I shook my head and was about to answer her when we heard Aja screaming. We looked at each other and then took off through the glass doors to see what was wrong. Ro stopped us and said, "She's okay. Just give her a few minutes. She must have been doing something she wasn't supposed to be doing." He was sitting down at the table chuckling.

Kia walked over and stood by the table, staring at him.

"What the hell did you do to my sister, Ro?" Kia asked.

He just laughed and started drinking his orange juice. Not one minute later, Aja came walking bowlegged like something was wrong with her. She had tears running down her face and her face was red. She had something red in her hands and threw it at Ro.

"I hate you, Ro! What the fuck was on it? My pussy is on fire! I have put water and everything on it and it won't stop burning!" she screamed, and was switching from foot to foot like she had to pee real badly.

I looked down and realized it was a big, red dildo that she threw at him, and now it was resting in the big platter of cheese eggs on the table.

Ro wiped his mouth with his napkin and said, "I told you, your freaky deaky ass was on punishment from coming. I knew your ass would be hard headed and try and use Big Red or your fingers to get that nut off. So, I rubbed jalapeno juice and cayenne pepper mixed together on your hands and Big Red. Then, I put some in the lube gel just in case that shit didn't work. I figured your disobedient ass wouldn't mind some hot ass pussy since you so hot in the ass to kill and torture motherfuckers. I made you a milk bath if you pull the shower curtains back. That should cool your pussy off and maybe next time you will listen to me. Now, carry your ass on before I make it another day of punishment."

She glared at him and stomped up the stairs with that bowlegged walk.

I heard her mumble, "I wish Viper was here. He wouldn't have done that shit to me! Might have had a sore pussy, but at least it wouldn't be on fire. Rude ass motherfucker!"

Ro shook his head and continued to eat. Kole, Kia, and I busted out laughing.

"Brah, why you do my sister like that? That was some evil shit! Do you know how much our hormones surge when we are pregnant? Now, times that by three and she has to be horny as hell. Please don't make my sister suffer," Kia joked.

"I'm not going to make her wait too long, but the shit she pulled last night could have gotten her and my babies killed. I need her to come off that Vixen shit until she drops my seeds," Ro said.

"Where's Tan?" I asked Kia, while I was making a plate of waffles. There was no way in hell I was touching those eggs now.

"He had to step out this morning and meet with some sources about Ray's whereabouts. I had a tracking chip in him, but he must have found it because it's not working. Tan knows someone that works for Doug and is not too happy. He's hoping he can get them to flip and provide us some information," she answered.

I nodded my head and asked about Big Kev.

"He's in there with Romero. After we ate, we headed in there to get some answers and dead his ass! That motherfucker so slimy I don't want to give him any chances to get away and go after my wife again. He's been fucking with her for too long. His life ends today, after he suffers," Ro stated.

The room got somber, and I knew all of us were thinking about all the shit that he had done to her

114

over the years. It was time to make his ass pay for what he did to her.

"Kole, the bat and barbed wire was a good choice. You have any other ideas?" Kia asked.

Kole looked at Ro and said, "Uh, Kia. That wasn't my idea. Your sister spoke to Big Kev, and he was following her orders. She said she wanted his dick ripped off from raping her and all the other women."

Ro shook his head and said, "Damn! See, how the fuck are my kids supposed to turn out normal when they mama is doing shit like that? My damn children gonna be serial killers in the fucking making. Let me go up here and talk to her ass. We will meet you in the basement in ten."

Ro headed upstairs, and we all finished eating and cleaning up. After dressing in the cloth suits we used for *playtime,* I was ready to work out my aggression and anger on Romero. The funeral was in two days, and I had to come up with a way to save Kyra and end this farce of a marriage I was being forced into. One way or another, I was getting my daughter back, and Camille and the rest of our enemies were going to pay, starting with Romero.

## Chapter 6- April

I had been trapped down in the basement for what seemed like days. One of the guys that they left to guard me got a phone call and ran out like the house was on fire. I figured something was going on because no one had been down to beat my ass or torture me in a few days.

When the guard returned, he told me that D-City Boyz had been taken over and I was free to go. He gave me his burner phone to keep and two hundred dollars and said I was on my own and left. I sat there for a minute, wondering if it was a trap. I decided I wasn't waiting around for someone to come back and finish the job that they had started. I went up the stairs and could tell that the house was empty.

I thought about the fact that Romero had left me to get caught and that my brothers hadn't even bothered to look for me. I didn't have anywhere to go and no one to count on. I figured that maybe there was something in the house that I could steal and pawn for money. Come hell or high water, I was getting the hell out of Nashville and never coming back! My so-called kids wanted me dead, and my man wasn't worth shit!

I went to the master bedroom and grabbed a pillowcase off the bed, but then I saw a suitcase on the floor and thought that might look less suspicious so I decided to put what I found to pawn in there. I searched the house and found jewelry, an iPad and Kindle, and a game system with some games. I figured that would at least get me five thousand dollars. That should get me to Atlanta, and then I could blend in and land myself a sugar daddy to take care of me. I looked in the closet and saw all the bad ass designer clothes that Aja had, and I figured I would take those too so I could dress the part once I got settled. I added the clothes to the growing pile on the bed and opened up the suitcase. Imagine my shock when I saw the suitcase was filled with money. It wasn't millions, but it looked like at least twenty or thirty thousand. I started twerking because my ass was set!

I used the burner phone to call a cab, but they said they wouldn't come out that far. I figured what the hell. I could just flag down a ride on the interstate and get them to drop me off at the bus station. I didn't want to take the chance of them confiscating my money at the airport. The bus people didn't give a damn.

I was happy the suitcase had rollers because I rolled it down the hill with me to the interstate below. I had put on one of my stolen dresses, a yellow bandage dress that hugged my curves. I knew it wouldn't be long before someone picked my fine ass up. I had washed up the best I could and covered my bruises with the makeup I found. I also cleaned the cuts on my stomach and bandaged them tightly. I also chewed on a few Tabs and was feeling a whole lot better.

It wasn't long after I stepped on the side of the interstate that a black Benz pulled up and rolled down the window. I stepped up to the window, making sure to push my breast up and bent over inside the window to see who was driving. He was okay enough to fuck. He looked like he was about forty-five or fifty with light skin and a grey and black beard.

"Hey handsome, can you give me a ride to the bus station?" I asked, making sure to bat my eyes.

He laughed and said, "Yeah, beautiful, as long as you ride something else before I drop you off."

I smiled and put my suitcase in the back seat. I got in the passenger seat and grabbed his crotch. He wasn't huge, but it felt like enough to keep a bitch happy. He smiled and then punched the shit out of me twice. I was shocked and trying to get out of the car door, but he must have had the child locks on. He punched me again and I saw stars. Blood was pouring from my nose and lips. He laughed at me and said, "Stupid bitch! You belong to me now!" He pulled off and my fate was sealed.

## Gena

I was finally able to get some time away from the house, and I was in my bae's bed getting my kitty serviced. Bae's tongue was lethal, and I had already had three orgasms and was working on my fourth. I felt two fingers being inserted into my treasure and bae started finger fucking the hell out of me. I felt another finger enter my ass. Between the tongue licking and sucking on my clit and fingers moving in and out of me, I knew I was about to explode.

"Damn, Lily. I'm about to cum, baby!" I yelled and squirted all over her face. She greedily licked it all up and kissed her way up my body. She licked my lips, and I opened my mouth to taste my juices on her tongue.

"Baby, that shit was everything. I can't wait for us to leave this country ass state so you can wake me up that way every morning," I said, smiling at the love of my life. She laid down on the pillow beside me and pulled my head on her shoulder and said, "We are almost there, baby. I am ready to retire and leave this shit for Camille to deal with. I have made Calvin's life a living hell and that is what I wanted to do. It's time for me to be happy, and I am most happy when I am with you."

I smiled because we had been messing around since I was nineteen. My father introduced us, and one thing led to another. We had been having an affair for the past four years. We were going to travel the world together and get married.

"Well, your plans worked out nicely. I am getting Ray to sign the papers today, and hopefully, he will be dead soon so I can collect my money," I said.

Lily started stroking my hair and replied, "You know I am a very rich woman. You didn't need his money, and you still don't. I promise I will take care of you."

I sighed because we always had this same argument. I never wanted her to think that I was with her for her money. My father's plan would make me a rich woman in my own right and show Lily that I could spoil her as much as she spoils me.

"Baby, you know how I feel about that. I love you, not your money. Soon, I will be rich and spoil you as much as you spoil me. I know they have the funeral set for two days from now. So, that means that all your enemies will be taken care of soon, and we can leave on Friday and head to the Maldives where we can lounge in our bungalow over the water and make love all day," I responded.

I heard my phone ping and thought it was my father because I hadn't heard from him and that wasn't normal, especially when payday was right around the corner. I looked at the phone and rolled my eyes. It was Ray asking where I was and if I could come and watch Rylei while he handled business. He was saying how much he loved me and couldn't wait for me to get home so he could show me. I couldn't wait for this shit to be over with because I couldn't stand his ass.

"Was that your loving husband?" Lily said with a chuckle.

"Yes, that was his stupid ass. He wants me to come home so I can watch Rylei. Hey, have you spoken with my father in the last few hours? He usually calls me and checks up on my progress, but I haven't heard from him," I asked.

"Gena, you know how your father gets. I am sure he is just fine. Romero has nine lives and hasn't used all of them up yet. He is probably laid up somewhere with your mama, April. You know those two are bound to get into anything," Lily replied.

I shook my head because I had the two craziest parents in the world. They sold me to a couple that just wanted the title of being parents. As soon as I was school age, they shipped me off to boarding school after boarding school. During my senior year, I found my adoption papers and went in search of my biological parents. Of course, it took several payments, stolen from my adopted parents, to get the real facts about my adoption because the papers were false. I found my mama first, and then she introduced me to Romero, and the rest was history.

They taught me everything I know about conning men out of money and setting people up. Romero introduced me to Lily, and she taught me how to manipulate men and become the woman of their dreams. She had the game on lock with her skills. I was her student, along with Camille, and we were the best at what we did. I had been able to afford a very nice lifestyle off the pockets of many rich men. Ray was my last big payday, and

I was excited as hell to put this chapter of my life behind me.

"Well, before I go, how about I taste that sweetness between your legs. I mean, it could be days before I see you again, and I need my fix," I said, as I kissed my way down her body and started pleasing my bae. Ray would have to wait.

## Chapter 7- Kia

We were about to go downstairs and beat some information out of Romero when we got the call that the infamous Corey and his brother were on the way to our location. I walked over to Tan who just got back from talking to the informant.

I wrapped my arms around his waist from behind and snuggled my face in his back. He turned around and sat down on the couch and brought me down on his lap. I could tell that something was bothering him, and I knew it had something to do with Ray.

"What's wrong, Tan? What happened with the informant?" I asked.

He cracked his knuckles, something he did when he was nervous or pissed off.

"The informant thought they had the address to the house where Ray was staying. But when I went to check it out, it was empty!" he said, and jumped up, making me fall back on the couch as he paced the floor.

"Kia, he has our daughter and she wasn't supposed to be without medical care until Doc cleared her. We don't know a damn thing about who this Gena person is. She could be some crazed killer, and the only thing he is thinking about is pussy. I swear when I catch his ass, I'm going to put a bullet in his fucking head.

I always knew he was a fuck boy, but I never knew he would be reckless with his own child!"

I got up and grabbed his face and looked at him in his beautiful brown eyes and said, "We will get our daughter back real soon. Then, we will make Ray and his hoe pay with their lives. You know how I give it!"

He stared at me for a moment and kissed me passionately on the lips.

I still couldn't do anything until my six weeks were up, but as soon as I healed, he was getting all the goodies!

We heard someone clearing their throat, and I looked up and saw a man that was the spitting image of my brother, Ace. The only difference was he was taller and had light brown eyes. There was no denying that my brother was his son. I just wondered how Ace was going to react to meeting his father with everything going on.

"Uncle Cordero? What the fuck are you doing here?" Tan asked.

I stood there in shock. What the hell did he mean uncle? Before I could ask some questions, Aja, Ro, Ace, and Kole came downstairs. Big Kev walked in with a man that I knew had to be Tan's father. The resemblance was uncanny except for the man had a darker skin complexion. His hair was a little past his shoulders and curly.

The others were looking between Tan and his father since they were involved in a stare down at the moment.

"Hello son, I see you are still upset with me and I understand. But we both have enemies that are causing problems, and we need to take care of them first and foremost," Tan's father said.

Tan just continued to stare until Cordero/Corey spoke up and said, "Tan, we need to talk to everyone now because we don't have a lot of time. We landed at a private airstrip, but we can't take the chance on staying here a long time. We've come to offer some help and some information because you are up against a powerful enemy, and you need backup in order to win. Swallow your pride, nephew, because your family will die if you don't listen."

Tan nodded his head and sat down on the couch. Everyone found a seat and waited to hear what was going on. Ace was the only one standing, staring at Cordero.

"So, I take it Corey or Cordero that you are my father. Why the hell would you leave me with April's crazy ass? Why are you here now?" Ace asked, while mean mugging Corey.

Corey sighed and responded, "Look, I know you have a lot of questions, but we really don't have time to answer everything right now until we take care of business. Long story short, I used to fuck around with April. I was in love with her and thought she loved me until I found out she was the neighborhood hoe.

When I found out she had given birth to you, I was in Cuba because my father was dying. I asked her for a blood test, and when I got the results back it said I wasn't your father, so I moved on. About five years ago, I got a call from Calvin and he said that he thought you were my son because you looked just like me. I called April and set up to meet with her one night and get to the bottom of the shit. When I got to the meeting spot, there was a body on the floor and I heard sirens. I barely escaped, but the bitch took pictures of me standing there with the body of a dead FBI agent. I am on the most wanted list here, so I try to stay in Cuba. When my cousin Anise called and gave me the code that Calvin and I made up, I knew you were in trouble and would need my help. Call me Corey by the way. I only use Cordero when I conduct business."

Ace shook his head and replied, "April is really a piece of work. I believe you because she has always been a snake. Whatever help you are offering, we will take it to get my daughter and niece back and kill these motherfuckers for good."

Corey walked over and hugged Ace.

"When this is over, I want you and your family to come to Cuba to meet the rest of the family. I also want to talk to you about a business matter, but that can wait. My brother, Anton, has a plan to help you out," Corey said.

Tan was still staring at his father, but Anton just shrugged it off and started speaking.

"Lily's family is deep into the Italian mob and that's where she gets most of her power. That is one of the reasons you are being hit from all sides. The good news is, I have spoken with the head of the family which is her uncle. They are not too happy with her because of the baby stealing business she has going on. Although they are criminals, they live by a code and follow it. They also don't like that she is a woman calling the shots. I was able to secure a promise from them that if anything happened to Lily and her daughter, there would be no retaliation against you or your families. They agreed, but they did have some stipulations that we have to discuss. I think their terms are fair, especially when it comes to your loved ones' safety."

Viper spoke up, and I knew it was crazy that I was starting to tell the difference.

"Look, we appreciate the help. My father spoke highly of you and your brother. I just didn't know the connection between you and Tan. I have a few friends coming to join us in a minute to help with the plan I spoke with you about on the phone. We will need all the help we can get. Let me go down to the basement and set everything up for my interrogation. It was nice to meet you, but I have to go and get in my zone," Viper said, as he left humming the theme song from Jeopardy. Big Kev followed behind him.

"I'm going to lie down for a minute. Kia, come and see me before it starts. I need to talk to you about something," Aja said. I could tell that she was up to something, and I am sure that Viper or Ro wouldn't be too happy.

That left Tan, Ace, Kole, and I to go over the plan with Corey and Anton. It was some devious shit, and it just might work if all the pieces fell into place. It's the first time I had seen my brother relax a little since Aciana was kidnapped. I just prayed that everything worked out as planned.

"We have to go soon before we are spotted, but Tan, I need to tell you and Kole something before I leave. I had to send your mama away because of the enemies I made in Cuba. I am not a perfect man. I had a mistress, and she was murdered brutally by my enemies. A month before she was killed, she bore me a son by the name of Kolson who you all know as Kole. I had Amelia take my son and leave him at the hospital in the states so he would not be killed also. I made sure that he was safe, and I watched from afar as I did you and Gunner. Even when you didn't see me, I was there for parties and graduations. I asked Rodney to put Kole on the Hit Squad so he could be close to his brothers. I know it's a lot to take in right now and there is a lot going on. I also want you all to come down to Cuba and spend some time there so I can explain everything that went down and is still going down. As a matter of fact, as I suggested to Viper, we must insist that you come after Lily and Camille are dead. There will be some of the mob that will seek retaliation, and you will need to lay low for a few months until my men can kill the rest. I promise you, Santano, that I will give you the answers you need. I just need you to give me a chance to make it up to you and your brothers. Kole, I'm sorry you had to find out this way about your family. I was just protecting my children," Anton said.

Kole stared down at Anton with so much anger that I just knew he was going to punch the hell out of him. Instead, Kole turned around and headed into the backyard and slammed the sliding glass doors so hard I thought they would shatter. The moment was interrupted by Corey's phone pinging, letting him know there was a message. He read it and said, "Anton man, we have to go. One of my FBI contacts said that they spotted our plane. Look, nephew, just make sure to get your friends and family out of the country as soon as the plan is over. Come down to Cuba and learn about your history and the rest of your family. Plus, there is also the matter of the terms that the Italians want in order for them to not retaliate against you and your family. It's very important that you agree and complete the tasks. If not, all hell will break loose and war will be declared. Ace, I love you, my son. Watch your back as well as your cousins and bring my granddaughter down to Cuba to meet me, as well as Kyra. Everything has been set in place by our people. Follow the plan and get out bottom line."

Corey hugged Ace and said his goodbyes. Anton stared out into the backyard at Kole and then back at Tan and said, "Santano, please watch over your brothers and yourself these next few days. A lot can go wrong with the plan if it is not followed down to the last detail. I hope to see you in Cuba, my son, as well as my granddaughters and your brothers. All I ask is that you give me a chance."

He walked over to me and grabbed my hands and said, "Akia, or should I say the Reaper, protect my sons as well as yourself. I see the way my son looks at you, and I know you have his heart. I need you to watch yourself. You have more enemies than you know about, young lady. I will explain more once you bring Sasha and Rylei to visit me in Cuba."

He kissed both my cheeks and headed towards the door behind Corey.

Before leaving out, he looked back at me and said, "I hope you live up to your reputation, Reaper. Because the bringer of death is exactly who you need to be in order to protect the people you love."

They left out of the door, and I turned around to see how Tan was taking everything that he had learned. He had sat down on the stool and looked at Ace.

"So, I guess we are family after all, cousin Ace. It's a good thing that you and Kia, don't share the same father, or I would be in trouble for messing with Kia," he chuckled.

I knew my baby was emotional because he always tried to crack a joke to cover up his emotions. All of us on the Hit Squad were trained to push our emotions down in order to live with what we did. Viper was the only one that had no regrets on taking lives, and we all knew why now. Kole came back in the door and sat down beside Tan.

"Tan, I hope you aren't upset about us being brothers. I know how much you love your mama, and I am the reason your parents split, according to our father. I always looked at all of you as brothers since I had no family growing up. Now, come to find out, you and Gunner are my brothers and Ace is my cousin. That shit has blown my mind," Kole said, shaking his head. Tan looked at Kole and smiled and replied, "Kole, man, you being my brother and Ace being our cousin, is the only good thing to come out of that conversation with our father. Shit, no offense, you can't help who your mama was or what she did. Hell, I don't even blame her because I know how shady my pops is. I need to call Gunner though and tell him what went down here."

Tan came and kissed me on the lips and headed out to the patio to call and talk to Gunner. Kole and Ace went down to the basement to help Viper set up so we could get rid of Romero, so he could never hurt my sister or another woman ever again.

But first, I had to go up and see what my sneaky ass sister was up to. I just hope I wouldn't have to cut Viper or Ro when they found out.

Chapter 8- Viper

I came downstairs to get my kill room together so I could finally make this motherfucker pay. It felt a little strange though getting ready to kill someone that looked like my pops. Every time I thought about my pops my heart hurt. I mean, this was the man that raised and loved me since I was a little man. Now, I was about to be a father and he wouldn't be here to give me any advice or to see his grandkids.

It pissed me off that my own brother was the one to do that shit. I know now that our father wasn't his biological father, but Rodney was the one that loved and raised his ass. On that point alone, he should have been grateful.

My head kept going to how to get at my brother because his ass had literally dropped off the face of the Earth. I knew that when I caught up with him that putting a bullet in his head would be hard because I loved him. His betrayal was so deep that it was fucking with my mental. I guess it was just the not knowing the reason why he did that shit. It was like his ass switched on the whole damn family all because of some bitch! I swear I couldn't wait to carve her fucking face off for all the trouble she had caused!

I needed to get all these motherfuckers that were fucking with us because Aja had started to do some sneaky shit. Not cheating or no shit like that, but she was on some kill or be killed type of shit. What she didn't know is in the next few days, we would be leaving the country. I had asked Kole to go down to Cuba to help set up houses for everyone down there. He was going anyways to get to know his family. I told him to put us close together so we could watch each other's backs, especially with all the kids that we had or would have coming soon.

I just wanted Aja to sit back and prepare for our seeds that would be coming soon. Doc and I had been talking, and he warned me that she would most likely deliver early because of there being three instead of one. My enemies had to be taken care of so I could marry Aja and find names for my seeds since she didn't like the ones I picked out. Hell, I didn't care if they were boys or girls because I would love them no matter what. I knew Aja would be an amazing mother and that was another reason I needed her ass to stop plotting.

She had turned straight savage on my ass. Now, in all honesty I wouldn't care as much if she wasn't pregnant. Shit, her bossing up was sexy as fuck to me and the trip thing was that she was really good at that shit. Her mind worked out angles of a plan like she was made for that shit. But, being pregnant and plotting murder was something I didn't want her doing. I needed to watch her more closely because I had a feeling I wasn't going to like what she was up to.

I really hoped this plan that Anton and Corey came up with worked and worked fast. It was time to get my affairs in order and create a life with me and my girl. I even have a proposition for her ass when she dropped my seeds. Hopefully, it would keep her occupied and also help her get those cravings for killing under control.

I laughed to myself because Pops would have loved her. The funeral was in a few days, and I didn't know how I was going to be able to say goodbye to him. I felt something on my cheek and realized it was a tear. Something I hadn't shed in years since my mama's murder. I pushed the emotions down and buried them.

I couldn't afford them right now, not with the enemies around me and the things that had to be done in order for the plan to work. I just prayed that we would all be standing afterwards. That's how dangerous it was.

**Chapter 9- Aja**

I had just finished taking another milk bath to calm down the burning that was still going on around my love button. I was still pissed that he went so far to make sure I didn't have an orgasm. I threw on some black leggings and pulled on one of Viper's black T-shirts to go over my growing belly. I couldn't believe I was about to be someone's mom, and not just to one, but three babies. I couldn't wait to meet them and spoil them rotten. I looked in the mirror, and I swear it looked like I was almost eight months pregnant instead of going on six months. I prayed that this plan worked because I really was sick of all the drama. I was ready to open my spa and marry my man.

I heard a knock at the door and I yelled come in. Kia walked towards me looking so beautiful. Her stomach was almost flat except for a small pudge. Rylei had done my sister's body good! She had more hips and breast than before, and her hair had gotten longer. I could see why Tan was so in love with her. My sister was a baddy! She also had on black leggings and what looked like Tan's shirt.

"Hey big sis, what the hell are you up to now so I can plan our funerals?" she asked with a smile.

I laughed along with her because she knew me well. Kyra had called me and let me in on the fact that Camille had gotten her phone number and text the invitation to her and Ace's wedding tomorrow. Kyra was so upset that she wanted to drive back to Nashville and whoop Camille's ass. I finally talked her down and talked to Doc about giving her something to calm her nerves. I really think that Camille was trying to make her lose her son. I filled Kia in on everything that Kyra had told me, and then I let her in on my plan.

"Bitch, we all gonna die tomorrow once your fiancés find out what the hell you are up to. You must like jalapeno coochie and no dick! Plus, your ass is good and pregnant with my nieces or nephews. Do you think I will risk their lives when I can easily do this shit by myself? Hell to the naw! Your ass will be sitting at this sham ass wedding until we can put the other plan in motion. See, Viper loves your ass, so you won't die. He likes me, so I might just get a quick death. I thought you loved your little sister, but you trying to get me caught up by your psycho ass baby daddies! Nope, nada, and no fucking way!" Kia yelled.

I looked at her with pleading eyes about to lay it on thick and said, "Kia, we made a promise when we were younger to always have each other's backs. You act like you are the only one that can protect the family. You know you can't get both of those bitches at the same time. You know my plan is the most effective way to make sure Aciana comes back to us safely. What happens if she gets caught in the crossfire, or they get word of the plan before we get there? This way, we can snatch her and get her back to Ace and Kyra without one hair on her beautiful head being harmed. Hell, they don't even have to know I had a part in it. I will play innocent like I didn't know a damn thing was going on. Come on, Kia. Let Vixen come out and play with Reaper. They can have Romero, Derrick, and Doug. We can take care of Camille, Lily, and Gena. You can fight Viper and Tan over who kills Ray. So what do you say, sis?"

Kia rolled her eyes and said, "If anybody finds out, I swear I am snitching on your ass! Now, come on so we can watch your future husband at work. I swear it is a thing of beauty."

I shook my head because she was just as bad as my fiancé. Tan had his hands full with her. On the way down, we talked about Rylei and how we were going to find her. As soon as we finished with our plan for tomorrow, we were going to get information from Gunner on Gena. The only thing

149

we knew about her was that she was fucking Ray and used to work at the chicken restaurant.

When we got in the basement, Ace handed us these cloth suits and we put them on over our clothes. I looked over at Romero chained to the ceiling all bloodied and bruised from the beating that I had Big Kev give him yesterday.

He was naked, and you could see the scabs from burns on him from the blowtorch that I asked Big Kev to use. His penis had huge chunks of meat missing and looked red and swollen like it was starting to get an infection. I had wanted that part of him to suffer the most. It was no telling how many women that he made suffer by raping and torturing them. He took the one thing that was supposed to be mine to give, my virginity. Then he stole my peace of mind and made me miss out on years with my family.

I looked over at Viper and he was staring at me as if he knew my thoughts. I was trying hard not to relive those moments, but it was hard to do with my stalker and rapist right in front of me. Viper walked over to me and pushed the hair out of my face. I leaned into his hand as he brushed it against my face making me feel better by just his touch.

"Baby girl if you not feeling this you don't have to be down here for it. I will make sure his last minutes on this Earth are nothing but pain for all the trouble he caused you. You can go upstairs and watch your ratchet TV and wait for me to come up and rub your feet," Viper said.

I shook my head no and replied, "I don't think I will truly have peace of mind if I don't watch him die. He has destroyed my life, security, and trust in people all because of his sick ass obsession with me. I am tired of him breathing the same air as me, and I want him to suffer. Then, I want you to kill him and burn the fucking body and put it in a dog pen so they can shit on it."

Viper busted out laughing like I had said the funniest shit ever. Hell, my ass was not playing. I was tired of his existence.

"Come sit right here, baby girl, and watch your man work. If at any time you need to leave, do so. I would rather you leave than stress my babies out," Viper said.

"That is my baby inside of her. Aja, tell him, baby, that you belong to me.

We are getting married as soon as the baby is born," Romero said, in a voice filled with pain.

Viper went over to the table and put on some gloves that had blades on them. They kind of reminded me of the superhero movie with the guy that had hands like claws.

"Uncle, do you know that blades are my favorite weapon of choice? Don't answer that because we both know you don't know me, and I don't give two fucks what you think anyways. Now, where was I? Oh, yes, blades. I love to use them because you get up close and personal when you use them. A gun is easy and impersonal. You can kill someone from a mile away with one and leave and eat your Coco Puffs. But with blades, you get up close to that person. See, Unc, you tried to take away the most important part of me; my heart. Aja never belonged to you because she was made for me. You have tortured her for years, and even violated her body because your ass is sick in the head. Any man that fucks his own sister deserves to die a slow death."

Viper swiped down Romero's chest so fast with the blades, I thought he missed until I saw his chest open up and blood start pouring from the wound. Viper poured a cup of some kind of liquid on the cut and Romero started screaming like he was on fire.

"Baby, what's in the cup?" I asked.

He smiled and came over and placed a kiss on my lips and said, "Look at you interested in your man's work. Keep that shit up, and I will take you off of punishment."

I sat straight up after hearing that. Hell, my pregnant, horny ass already had juices flowing just thinking about the dick. I needed it, and if asking questions would get me dicked down, hell, I'd be Barbara Walters for that dick!

"But, baby girl, to answer your question, it's a mixture of salt, lemon juice, and hot sauce. It took me a few months to come up with that recipe for the right amount of pain. So right now, he feels like he is on fire. So that's why his bitch ass is screaming," Viper replied.

He went over to Romero and started slicing him some more like he was carving up a Thanksgiving turkey. We all sat around and watched in amazement at how Romero looked now. He looked like someone had sliced off most of his skin, and you could see his muscles and tendons. His breathing was getting labored, and I could tell he was suffering. Every time he was sliced, Viper would throw the mixture in the wound. Romero was sobbing and begging to die. The man that had fucked up my life was getting fucked up himself.

Viper walked over to the table and took the gloves off. He walked over to me with blood all over his cloth suit. He stood in front of me sweaty and chest heaving from the work he had put in on Romero. He grabbed me and tongued my ass down like we were at the altar. He slowed down and placed small kisses on my lips. I swear my damn panties were flooded. He kissed me on the side of the neck, making his way up to my ears and started nibbling them.

He then whispered, "Baby girl, he no longer has any power over you. His ass will never again breathe the same air as you. Tell daddy what you want me to do next to make him suffer."

He then proceeded to lick my ear and make his way down my neck.

"Man! I'm out! Viper, man, you don't see us all standing here while you freaking on my damn sister? Let me know when he's dead. I'm going upstairs to have a beer," Ace said, leaving out.

There was a chorus of "me too's" and everyone left. I looked at Viper and he was staring at me with so much lust. I wanted him so bad, I just couldn't wait.

I started tearing the cloth suit off of him, and he did the same with mine. He helped me get out of my leggings and pulled his t-shirt over my head. I didn't have on any undergarments under it so I was standing before him naked. He pulled down his basketball shorts he had on under the suit and his big beautiful third leg sprang up and damn near made me drool. He picked me up and placed me on the empty table over to the side and pulled me to the edge. He rubbed a finger down my slit and

156

felt all the juices that I know were running from me with every touch. He stared down at me and said, "I love you, baby girl."

I started to reply but couldn't get it out before he entered me in one stroke.

I gasped because I wasn't prepared for the pleasure-pain mixture. He pulled me down farther to the edge of the table and had my legs resting in the crook of his arms. He started off with slow, grinding, circular strokes that were driving me crazy. The way he was doing it had him grazing my clit, but not directly touching it.

I was moaning whenever his pelvis would lightly touch it. Viper was staring at me with an intensity I had never seen before. I also realized that the torture had turned him on some way, and instead of being sickened or turned off, it turned me on more. I guess I needed to go see his doctor, too.

I heard someone sniffle and I immediately looked over and met Romero's eyes. Hell, I forgot he was there. I guess watching Viper fucking me was getting to him.

"Oh, shit!" I said, as Viper took his dick out to the tip and plunged back in. When I looked at him, he had a scowl on his face and said, "When I am in my pussy, I am the only motherfucker you better be looking at! Fuck him! This is my pussy, and he needs to watch his worst nightmare before I kill him. I want me fucking you to be the last image in his mind before I send him to hell."

He then started giving long, deep strokes, alternating between fast and slow.

"Oh, fuck. Viper, that feels so damn good!" I moaned.

"Shit baby girl, you got the best pussy I ever had! Your walls are wringing this nut out of me," he replied.

Just his voice saying the word nut sent me over the edge, and I started squirting so hard I was seeing stars. My body was so sensitive that as soon as I felt Viper's semen spurt inside of me, I started cumming again.

When I opened my eyes, Romero was staring at me with tears streaming down his face. He looked pathetic, and I smiled. Viper reached over and grabbed the gun that was on the shelf beside us and put a hole in Romero's head, sending blood splatter on my naked body and his. I felt his dick that was still inside me growing hard as hell.

Oh well, let me enjoy this ride before I was back on dick punishment after I put my plan in motion. It would be worth it to get rid of those two bitches.

## Chapter 10 - Aja

I woke up well satisfied and refreshed. My baby had put in work most of the night, making up for lost time. I was deliciously sore all over my body, both inside and out. I moved away from Viper who was asleep so I could get up and take care of my hygiene and fix everyone some breakfast. Plus, I needed to make a phone call that would help put my plan in motion.

After showering, I threw on a t-shirt dress and headed downstairs. I mixed some blueberry muffins and put them in the oven to bake. I already had sausage and bacon cooking on the stove, and had cut up some melons that were chilling in the fridge. I decided I was just going to boil some eggs because I didn't feel like frying them.

I sat down at the island and texted Gunner, asking him to send me Camille's number. After waiting a few minutes, he sent me the number and I started dialing.

"Hello?" she answered.

I took a deep breath so I could give the performance of a lifetime and said, "Hi, Camille. This is Aja. I know the wedding is in a few hours, and I just wanted to see if you needed Kia and me to do anything since you asked us to be bridesmaids and all."

She started laughing and replied, "Bitch, please! You could care less about what I need. You should be happy I even invited you and your crazy ass sister to the wedding. Now, what the fuck do you really want?"

"Camille, look, I am just trying to keep you happy so that Ace can see his daughter. I overheard him last night talking to Ro and telling him that he wished that Aciana could be there. You know how serious that Ace is about family events since we had a fucked up upbringing. Even though you are forcing him to marry you, he is taking it very seriously. I figured if I could make

161

the day less stressful for you, that maybe you would let Aciana see her father before he gets married. That's why I am willing to put my dislike of you aside in order for my niece and brother to be together. It's not about us or anyone else. Plus, you are carrying my niece or nephew. I love my family, and you are bringing a new member into it soon. We have to learn to get along for their sake," I answered.

There was silence for a few minutes, and I was wondering if I had laid it on too thick.

"Okay, Aja. I will bring Aciana to the chapel for the ceremony. However, she will not be at the reception that I put together. I don't want to give her the wrong impression since alcohol will be passed around. I mean, I am her mother now and have to set a good example," Camille responded.

I gritted my teeth because I really wanted to cuss her ass out, but on the strength of getting my niece away from this crazy bitch, I let her slide.

"Great. Camille, thank you. Do you have a hairdresser or makeup artist? I know a few people I could call for you. That way, you could just sit back and relax and enjoy your day," I asked.

Camille answered quickly. "Yes, of course. I have my own team from JaBelle coming to beat my face and make sure my hair is on point, so you don't have to worry about that. I even have me something new, blue, and all of that. I just need you to wear a glamorous red dress and make sure that your tomboy sister does, too. Now, if you will excuse me, sister-in-law, I have to go run an errand before I walk down the aisle. Goodbye."

I ended the call and sat and thought about what I had accomplished. I heard footsteps and saw Kia and Tan coming down the stairs. I stared at Kia and gave her the thumbs up. She nodded and headed towards the table to sit down in the chair.

"So, sis, you like fucking in front of people," Kia stated, and Tan and her cracked up laughing.

"Really Kia, you just had to go there? I seriously just forgot his ass was in there. I was enjoying the moment with my man and not thinking about Romero's crazy ass. Plus, Viper's ass wanted that to be another form of torture, and his crazy self wouldn't stop. Oh, did you call the cleanup crew to come and pick up the body?" I asked.

Tan spoke up and said, "Sis, I called them, and they should be here in about an hour. Viper wanted them to come yesterday when Anton and Corey were here, but something came up with them, and they couldn't make it. We need to make sure they are prepared to help us with the plan tomorrow. Plus, Zontae owns the funeral home where the services will be held. He just wants to go over everything that you all talked about in the email concerning Rodney and Ms. Shelly. Just don't stare at them too hard, especially Zontae."

I scowled at him and said, "Why is he that ugly or something?"

Kia started laughing, and it was Tan's turn to scowl.

"Aja, that nigga is fine as fuck! He was the color of coffee with lots of cream, a nice trimmed beard, and the body of a linebacker. The only thing I can't deal with is he wears sunglasses all the fucking time. His ass never takes them off, talking about his eyes is sensitive to the light," she replied.

Tan said, "So you really want to fuck Zontae or something? I mean you over here talking about another man like I'm not standing here. Keep fucking with me and watch and see if I don't spank your ass!"

Kia laughed and said, "Shit. Daddy, I might like that shit!"

Tan didn't laugh, so I guess he didn't find it as funny as we did.

Kia went and wrapped her arm around Tan and said, "Santano, baby, you have nothing to worry about. I only have eyes for a certain Cuban who gets on my damn nerves," Kia said, and pecked him on the lips.

I took out the muffins and started setting everything up on the table so everyone could eat. I told Tan to go and wake everyone up. As soon as he left, I filled Kia in on my conversation with Camille. I texted Gunner and had him set up a few things; I made up a story about tying up some loose ends so he wouldn't snitch and tell my fiancé. The doorbell rang, and I told Kia to watch the last of the bacon that was cooking.

Big Kev was already at the door, and when it opened, I swear I stopped breathing. Standing before me were two of the prettiest men I had ever seen. One was leaner with a low cut fade, hazel eyes, and was the definition of a pretty boy. He had a friendly smile on his face and was chatting with Big Kev. The other man was sexy as hell, and had that *don't give a fuck attitude* about him. I couldn't see his eyes because he was wearing some very dark sunglasses. By the description, this one must be Zontae. They both had on black joggers and black tank tops. Their muscles and tattoos were on full display, as well as those big ass prints below.

I was about to speak before I was snatched back into a hard chest and a muscular arm went across my neck. My nose was instantly invaded by the Irish spring soap that he used. Damn! A bitch couldn't catch a break! I wasn't going to sample from the menu because I loved my man too much for that. But hell, I just wanted to browse and look at all the delicious entrees on the menu.

"Take your ass in the kitchen! That's the second fucking time I have caught you staring at another nigga's dick. Keep that shit up and see if I don't lock your ass up until you have my seeds!" Viper yelled in my ear.

I carried my embarrassed ass right on in the kitchen and started fixing my man's plate while mean mugging Kia for laughing.

"Bitch, you could have warned me that he was coming down the stairs! You supposed to be my sister and watch out for me. Now, his ass is going to be on a hundred with his attitude," I whispered so only she could hear.

"Aja, nobody told your ass to stare that long at Zontae and Mesa. Hell, what am I saying? The reason I didn't say anything was because my ass was too busy staring from the doorway, and he was already headed your way," Kia replied.

We both started laughing and getting everything together for breakfast. The men came in and sat down at the table minus Zontae and Mesa. I wanted to ask where they were, but the look on Viper's face told me to shut my ass up and eat.

After breakfast, we all went upstairs to get dressed for the fake wedding. I refused to acknowledge it as a real one. I pulled my hair into a neat bun in the back and put on this red flowing chiffon, baby doll dress. I put on some gold and red wedges and got ready. I left my face bare since Camille wanted us all to get our makeup done by the JaBelle staff. Viper was moving around the room getting dressed in the black tuxedo the guys all were wearing for the wedding. He still wouldn't talk to me. I went and wrapped my arms around his back and he just stood still. He turned around and we stared at each other for a few minutes. He lowered his face to mine and kissed me on the lips. I threw my arms around his neck and the kiss grew deeper. We reluctantly pulled apart and headed downstairs to load up the cars to head to the wedding from hell.

## Chapter 11- Camille

I was standing in my silk robe with my La Perla, white, bridal set on underneath, waiting on everyone to arrive. I smiled at myself in the mirror, thinking that I was finally getting my man. I looked at the little pudge in my stomach and couldn't wait for our baby to be born.

I looked over at Aciana who was asleep on the chaise lounge. I had every intention of selling her and collecting the huge payday, but after spending time with her, I realized that she was a sweet child and could be molded to what I wanted her to be. Since I wanted the baby I was carrying to be a boy, I figured that I could save my figure and just adopt Aciana. She would be my daughter, and I could teach her how to be a boss bitch just like my mama taught me.

The drug business that we stole from D-City was making more than enough money for me to retire from the baby selling business. With my last shipment of babies being dropped off at the FBI headquarters, we had to lay low because that one incident had garnered a lot of attention. I contacted my European contacts just this morning and sold all my contacts for the baby selling business. I now was a cool eight million dollars richer.

There was a knock on the door, and the hairdresser, makeup artist, and wedding coordinator all stepped in. I had to pay an extra two hundred thousand for this private wedding on short notice. Two days wasn't long to pull my dream wedding off. Luckily, I had my dream wedding dress created a year ago. It was a custom Pnina Tornei, diamond encrusted, Grecian-style gown. It was loose enough for my stomach, but had a dramatic high and low chiffon bottom with the train trailing behind. Real diamonds were sprinkled all over the gown, especially the bodice and train. It was designed to hang off of one shoulder with the diamond straps. It cost me well over two million dollars, but it was so worth it. I would sparkle all the way down the aisle to my husband. I had made it my mission to be married to Ace by the end of the year. Look at me now. I have an empire, two children, and soon, I would be tied to the man I love in matrimony.

There were two people that I really wanted to share this with, but neither one were here on my special day. I hadn't heard from Tyesha in months, and I knew that something had to have happened to her. She was a good mother and never wanted to be away from her kids. I had been going over to Derrick's and checking on Dajae and Daria as much as I could.

I instantly felt bad about the shit I had been doing behind her back. Derrick and I had been fucking for the past four months since she had been gone. To be honest, I wasn't sure if the baby I was carrying was Ace's or his. If I had to kill Derrick in order to keep my secret, then that is exactly what I would do. Because no matter what the DNA said, Ace was the father of my little one.

The second person I was missing was my mother. She was still upset that I wouldn't kill Ace. When I told her about the wedding, she refused to be a part of it. So, I spent the past forty-eight hours planning my wedding by myself.

The hair stylist and the makeup artist had just finished with my hair and makeup when Aja came in looking like a maternity model in a beautiful, red, baby doll dress and some red wedges. She sat down in the chair by the door and said, "Well, Camille, I must say that you make one beautiful bride. I love the hair and makeup. I mean, in the words of the great Madea, you are casket sharp."

She started giggling, and I chose to ignore her. Nobody was ruining my special day.

"Tee Tee, I missed you!" I heard Aciana say. I guess she had woken up from her nap. I watched as she ran to Aja and jumped in her arms. The bitch better enjoy my daughter while she could, because by tomorrow night, she would be dead along with her crew.

"Aciana, Does Mommy look pretty?" I said to her.

"You are very pretty. But, Ms. Camille, my mommy's name is Kyra. Tell her, Tee Tee, because I think Ms. Camille picked up the wrong girl by mistake," Aciana replied.

I saw Aja smile with a smug look on her face. I opened the bottle of water to take a sip because my mouth was tingling and a little numb. I was still having morning sickness, so I figured I might be having another bout soon. I looked in the mirror and noticed my lips were swollen. I told the makeup artist earlier that I would need hypo-allergenic. You would think with as much money as I paid them that they would not use the cheap shit!

I was about to reach for my cell phone and call them and demand to speak to their manager, but something was off. I was trying to move but it felt like my arms were dead weight. I looked in the mirror again and my lips were three times bigger than before and drool was running out of the sides of my mouth. I looked in the mirror and saw Aja staring at me and smiling. That bitch had done something to me.

"Aciana, baby, it's time for you to put your beautiful white dress on so you can toss the flower petals. Go behind that screen and get dressed. Even when you finish, just wait there until Tee Tee comes to get you. I brought my Kindle so you can play games on it. Here, put the earbuds in so you don't miss anything. Okay, baby girl?" Aja asked Aciana. Aciana nodded her head yes and skipped over behind the screen.

My stomach started cramping so bad I thought that I thought I would pass out. I watched as my lips swelled so big I thought they would burst. Tears were coming from my eyes, and I was able to mumble, "What did you do to me?"

Aja smiled and said, "Hold on a minute. Don't die yet. A very important bridal party member is waiting to speak with you.

She walked to the door and opened it up; standing there looking just like a chocolate goddess was Kyra. Her face was beat to the gods and her hair was in large barrel curls falling down her back with a braid going across the top in a perfect Grecian style. Her gray eyes narrowed in on me, and she walked over to me and slapped the shit out of me. More tears poured down my face and my body felt like it was on fire. I felt a gush on my panties and knew I was losing my baby. Kyra went and sat in the chair that Aja had occupied, rubbing her pregnant belly.

Aja bent down in front of me and my vision doubled as her face swam in front of me. It was getting harder to breathe, and the pain was becoming unbearable. I prayed that it would end soon.

"Well, Camille, I told you that you were casket sharp today. You see my fiancé is something of a torture connoisseur. He had all kinds of goodies in his kill bag. I was looking for something that would make you feel every single part of your body in pain. I found what he calls his Viper juice. It's a mixture of Black Mamba, Pit Viper, and Cobra venom. Now, don't ask me how I got it because you really will be dead before I have a chance to tell you the story. I switched out the Botox injection that you asked for with the venom to get those skinny ass lips of yours plump for the wedding. I also paid the staff to bring you venom water so I could ensure that you died. Simply put, you fucked with the wrong family, and now you have to die," she said and walked over to Kyra.

I could already feel myself getting weaker, and I was now foaming at the mouth and nose. I was dying and wished that my mother was here so I could see her one last time.

Kyra walked over and stood in front of me shaking her head. She looked at me with a smile and said, "Just know that your hard work with the wedding won't go to waste. I am going to walk my beautiful pregnant ass down the aisle in that expensive dress and marry the man that I love. We will make love in the hotel suite you paid for, and I will be giving birth to his son in a few months. All the things you thought you had taken from me were never yours to begin with. Now, rot in hell you stupid ass bitch!"

Kyra walked away and grabbed the wedding dress that I thought I would be getting married in and stepped behind the screen. I heard her and Aciana talking and saw that they were hugging in the silhouette. I was punched and fell out of the chair. I looked up and Aja was standing over me as my vision slowly faded. The last thing I heard was Aja's voice saying, "Don't worry. Your mama will be joining you in hell soon, so you won't be lonely."

Those were the last words I heard before my world and my life went dark.

## Ace

I was standing at the end of the aisle waiting for this shit to be over with. Ro had made an appearance in the dressing room, so he and Tan were standing with me at the altar. Camille had gone all out with this fucked up wedding. The whole chapel had blackout curtains so that the inside was dark. The only light were the lights from the hundreds of candles in different sizes around the altar and aisles. There were white roses everywhere, decorating every inch of the place. I swear it looked like some type of fairy tale garden that was in one of Aciana's books.

I heard the music playing and saw Kia and Aja walking down the aisle side by side in red, flowing dresses. My sisters were so beautiful, and my cousin and best friend were very lucky men. They both had smiles on their faces and tears in their eyes. I frowned at their asses because this was not a real fucking wedding. A real wedding would be watching my soul mate walk towards me with love and tears of joy in her beautiful gray eyes.

The music changed to John Legend's song "All of me". I really wanted to kill this bitch because that was Kyra's favorite song, and it made me feel bad as hell to be going through with this when she was the one meant to be my wife.

The doors opened, and my beautiful daughter walked, well ran down the aisle to me. She wrapped her arms around me and I held on tight. I couldn't believe that Camille allowed her to be here. I didn't want to let her go, but she pushed me away and said, "Daddy, I have to go back and throw the flowers for the bride!"

She ran down the aisle throwing flowers everywhere. She lightened the dark mood that I had been in. After she finished, she ran over to her Tee Tee Aja and grabbed her hand. I wanted to go and grab my daughter and hold on tight because I didn't know when Camille would let me see her again.

I was brought out of my thoughts when I heard my boys gasp. I looked in the direction that they were staring in and saw that the doors had opened, and the most beautiful sight stood before me. She was my all, and she stood at the beginning of the aisle looking like a sparkling angel. Her hair was flowing down her back, her breasts were sitting up right, and her curves were outlined in the white dress that looked like a floating cloud.

As she started down the aisle, I swear it looked like she was gliding down to me. I didn't know it until it hit my hand, but tears were falling from my eyes watching the woman that I loved walk towards me.

She finally stood in front of me with those beautiful, glowing gray eyes with tears running down her face. I put my hand on her round belly and felt my son kick. I don't know how the hell she got here, and right now, I didn't care. She was leaving here with my last name, and I would kill anyone that tried to stop it.

"Hi, baby, are you happy to see me?" she asked.

I smiled into her eyes because I was more than happy to see her. Hell, I was overjoyed to see my baby at the altar with me.

"Of course Ky, I never wanted to marry anyone else but you," I replied.

I was about to kiss her when the minister cleared his throat so we could get the vows started.

"Well, since I haven't spoken with the new bride on what she wants as far as vows, I think it's best that you both speak from your hearts," the minister said.

Kia sent Aciana over to grab Kyra's bouquet. We grabbed each other's hands and smiled at each other.

Kyra took a deep breath and said, "Ace, when I first met you, I literally felt my heart stop. I tried to fight the connection we had, because you were my best friend's brother, but you wouldn't take no for an answer. You make me feel so loved and protected. You are my one, and I will never let anybody get in the way of our love ever again. You are my rock, and I promise to always trust and love you. I make this commitment to you to be a wife, lover, and constant companion for as long as we both shall live. I love you, Ace, and I can't wait to spend the rest of my life with you."

I wiped the tears that were flowing from her eyes as she said her vows to me. I'm not even gonna lie, I had a few tears flowing as well. I kissed her hand and looked into her eyes.

"Ky, baby, what you don't know is that I noticed you when you first moved into our neighborhood. You were fussing with the movers because they dropped your TV and broke it. Now,

I was laughing because your short ass was really going in on them. But, I admired your feistiness and fearlessness. Your young ass had me sprung! I would peep out the window and watch you sit on your porch with your head in those books. I thought to myself that I needed to step my game up if I wanted to be with you. You were the first female to ever make me want to be better. When I look at you, I don't just see my wife, I see my best friend. Those years apart really broke a nigga down and put me in a dark place. I promised that if I ever got you back that I would lock you down forever. I am ready to give you and our kids my time, love, and all of me. I promise to put y'all first and to give you not only the world, but my heart and soul. Kyra, I love you and can't wait to spend the rest of my life with you," I promised.

"Alright, do you have the rings?" the minister said.

I smiled because when I went to pick up the ring I was giving Camille, I saw a 10-karat, heart shaped diamond that was perfect for Kyra. My baby had a thing for hearts.

I pulled out the ring and placed it on her finger. Ro had my ring because my sisters had been MIA right before the wedding. Kyra placed it on my finger, and I felt like the darkness that I felt earlier disappeared.

"Kyra and Ace, you have expressed your love to one another through the commitment and promises you have just made. It is with these in mind that I pronounce you husband and wife. You may kiss the bride."

I grabbed my wife and poured all my love into that kiss. I felt a tug on my leg and looked down to see my baby girl smiling up at me. I picked her up and shifted her into one arm. I grabbed my wife's hand with the other. I came in the chapel to marry the devil, but instead, came out with two angels.

# Chapter 12- Aja

I was so happy for my brother and my best friend! I cried like a baby, and it wasn't just these pregnancy hormones. They had been through hell and still came out on the other end stronger and together. I had called Zontae and Mesa and they came and got Camille's body so they could make it disappear. Getting rid of Camille was the first part of my plan. Now, we had one more part to go on my plan. My fiancé would take care of the rest of them.

We had all went out to eat afterwards to celebrate Ace's and Kyra's marriage. We then saw the happy couple off as they headed to the hotel to get some much needed alone time. I asked Kyra if she wanted me to keep Aciana, but she said that she wanted to keep her baby close.

We were headed back to the safe house with Kia and Tan. Kole had to go down to the cabin to help Gunner out with a problem. I noticed that Ro kept sneaking glances at me. The stares were starting to make me uncomfortable. It felt like he could see that I was hiding something. His ass was too damn quiet. Then, I thought about it. Tan's ass was quiet, too. I looked at Kia in the rearview mirror and we shared a look.

As soon as we pulled up to the house, Kia and I jumped out and went to the kitchen.

"Kia, did you get to get the info?" I whispered.

"Yeah, we can go tonight after they are asleep. I am just ready to cut the head of the snake. Now, take your ass upstairs because Tan and Ro are acting strange, and I don't like it. I will meet you in the backyard at 2 a.m., and make sure you where something dark," Kia said.

I headed upstairs, and Ro was not in the room. I figured that he was down in the basement with Tan. I took my shower and threw on a t-shirt so I could get a little bit of sleep before I had to sneak out with Kia. I climbed in the bed and started drifting off.

You ever been asleep and felt like someone was watching you. Well, that's what made my eyes pop open and found myself staring into a pair of angry light brown eyes. I jumped up and scooted to the headboard because he was sitting there holding some type of snake.

"Viper, why the hell are you sitting here with a snake in your lap, staring at me? This is some creepy shit even for you!" I yelled.

He just sat there rubbing this big ass snake like it was a damn puppy.

He continued to stare and about two minutes later he said, "I have never been in a real relationship before, and I know you haven't either. The problem that I am having is the trust you are supposed to have in your man. I mean, if you can't trust me then why in the fuck are we together?"

He started rubbing that damn snake again, and I swear the snake's eyes were mean- mugging my ass.

"Baby, of course I trust you! I love you, and you have done nothing but be a good man to me. Please, baby. What is this about?" I asked.

He started chuckling and moved with the snake to the foot of the bed and replied, "Aja, I don't like people to lie to me or omit the truth. I expect nothing but honesty from my wife. I want to be her partner in everything. I want her to come to me when she is plotting and doing shit that can get her and my children killed. Now, I don't want you to say shit right now because your ass will just lie. From now on, you can't leave this house without me being with you. So, you can squash that little sneaky shit that you and Kia have going on tonight. Tan and I will take care of it. Now, since you seem to have a thing for snakes, remember if you try to do some more sneaky shit, you will be bathing with these motherfuckers, and I know for a fact that you don't want that shit. Now, pick up the papers on the nightstand and sign them. Don't read the shit just sign every page since you say you trust me."

Of course I picked up the pen and signed and initialed every damn line. I probably just signed a damn death contract or some shit. My fiancé wasn't looking too stable right now with that damn snake. The door opened, and Tan came in dressed in all black with two men in a suit I didn't recognize.

"Give the first set of papers to Ebb. He's my accountant," Viper said.

The man named Ebb took the papers and looked them over and left. I guess he had what he needed. All this shit was strange as fuck to me, but what the hell was I supposed to do about it. This crazy ass nigga had a gun in his back, blades in his pockets, and let's not forget the damn big ass snake that was looking at me like I was its next meal. I don't know how he found out, and I think that was what was scaring me the most.

The other guy looked over the papers and said, "Do you agree to everything these papers say?" He asked.

I nodded my head and said, "Yes, I agree."

The man gave the papers over to Viper and he signed them also. I was scared because I didn't know what the hell I had just signed. Viper passed the papers back to the man, and Tan handed him an envelope and they both left out of the door.

I was waiting for Viper to say something, but he just continued to rub that ugly ass snake. He finally stood up and put the snake on the dresser. He leaned over me and placed a kiss on my forehead and said, "Baby girl, I love that you want to look out for your family and friends. But, you also have a husband that will help you take care of them. If you had told me about your plan, I would have agreed to it because it was perfection. You made that bitch suffer with very little bloodshed. I couldn't have planned it better myself. I found out about your plan when Zontae and Mesa called, bragging about you fucking her ass up. Now, imagine how I felt when another man called and told me something I didn't know about my wife. I don't give a fuck if you think I will say no or go off. Sometimes, I might surprise you and say yes. Do you understand what I am saying, Aja Lanae Casey?"

I nodded my head yes and smiled. I loved that he just used the name I would receive when we got married.

"Now, I need you to agree that when we get married, you will listen to what I say and try and follow my lead. Remember, you told me before that the husband was the king and the wife listened to her king. That is what you said, right?" he asked.

I responded, "Yes, baby. You will be my king, and I will listen. I promise."

Viper smiled and kissed me, and I instantly got wet. Damn, his kisses made me weak as hell. Unfortunately, he ended the kiss with a few sweet pecks and said, "Close your eyes, baby. I have something that I want to give you. I have to go and take care of the other part in your plan. I need you to stay here and just chill out until I get back. As soon as you hear the door close, count to fifty. Can you do that for me?"

I nodded my head yes and he placed another sweet kiss on my lips and forehead. I heard paper rattling and his footsteps leaving out. I started counting to fifty and wondered what the surprise could be. I must admit, I was relieved to just let go and let him take care of the rest of the enemies we had. I needed to get ready for these babies to be born and figure out what I wanted to do with myself once they were born. I got to fifty and opened my eyes. Thank God he took that creepy ass snake with him!

I looked on the pillow beside me and there was a blue velvet ring box. I smiled, wondering what new piece of jewelry my man had gotten me. I opened the case and was almost blinded by a beautiful platinum ring with diamonds encircling the entire ring. I almost cried when I read the inscription. It read *our love beats all.* I slid the ring on to see how it would look on the day he would place it on my hand. I almost forgot the two pieces of paper lying to the side.

I looked down at the large piece of paper and immediately wanted to beat the shit out of Viper! His ass tricked me, and I fell for that shit!

I looked at the smaller note and it said:

*"You might as well slide that ring on Mrs. Roland Symir Casey. You are my wifey now!"*

I let out a scream from the top of my lungs! Who the fuck tricks somebody into marrying them just so they would follow directions? Oh, yeah. That would be my crazy ass husband!

# Chapter 13- VIPER

Tan, Kia, and I were in the driveway about to leave, when we heard Aja scream. Kia started running towards the front door until I stopped her.

"She's okay, Kia. She just got some news she wasn't expecting," I said, laughing.

Tan looked at me and shook his head because he knew what I had just done so he was laughing too and said, "Viper, man, you dirty as hell doing that girl like that!"

"Okay, you assholes. What did you do to my sister, Viper? I thought you said you wouldn't hurt her if I told you her plan," Kia asked.

"Okay, I'll tell you in the car. Let's go before your crazy ass sister comes out here and hits me in the balls with a bat or some shit. I think I have rubbed off on her and that shit is starting to scare me," I replied.

We all piled in the car with Big Kev. He was going to be our driver in case we needed a quick escape. As soon as we were on the interstate, Kia said, "Okay. Can somebody please tell me now why my sister was screaming before we left?

I responded, "Yeah, I tricked her into getting married."

"What the hell? That doesn't make any sense. She already agreed to marry you," she answered.

Tan spoke up and said, "No, baby. This fool made her sign the marriage certificate and paid a judge to come and oversee the ceremony. Now, mind you, Aja had no clue what was going on because his ass had her shook by petting a fucking snake and acting crazier than normal."

I laughed and said, "Shit, she said she would listen to me if we were married, and I had to do something to keep her savage ass in control. So, I left the marriage certificate on her pillow along with the wedding band. She's now Mrs. Casey, so problem solved. I had Ebb come so she now gets everything in case something happens to me. Hell, we at war right now, and the plan for tomorrow is very dangerous. I needed to make sure that she and my seeds would be well taken care of."

Kia popped me in the back of the head with her hand, and that shit hurt.

"Hey Kia, watch your fucking hands! You sis and all, but I will fuck you up if you hit me again," I said, laughing at the same time.

"Viper, you have really fucked up now. Do you know that Aja has been dreaming about her wedding since she was eight? Now, you have just taken that away from her. I understand wanting to make sure she's safe and your kids are taken care of, but you petty as hell for doing that to my sister! I hope she fucks you up when you get back to the house!" Kia yelled.

I hadn't really thought about that. I didn't mean to ruin her dreams and shit. Well, then again, I was trying to be petty as hell when I found out she was trying to sneak out tonight with her pregnant ass to go and kill somebody. I needed to fix this shit fast. I dialed Kole's number and asked him to put Ms. Anise on the phone. I told her what I did, and she cussed my ass out! Kia's instigating ass was laughing because you could hear every word Ms. Anise said, because I had accidently hit the speakerphone button. I told her I was sorry and needed her help with planning something for my baby when we got to Cuba. I told Gunner to give Anise my black card I left with him in case of emergencies.

Calvin was awake and doing better, but he would need physical therapy, so I set up a private one for him in Cuba. Anise, Calvin, and Kole would be moving down to Cuba to wait on us until we got there. Kole told me that Anton had found a compound that had six houses on it with a top of the line security system.

I finished my call with Ms. Anise and felt better about the situation. I might have to watch my back for a few days, but it would be well worth it once she hit Cuba and saw her surprise.

We pulled up to the hotel that Gunner sent me the coordinates to. Somehow, my beautiful wife had stumbled upon information on Lily. Apparently, she came to this hotel once a week to meet up with someone. I had called in some favors and put together a small crew of loyal friends. Zontae, Mesa, and Arco were already positioned around the hotel to make sure that if we got in trouble, we would have backup. Tan, Kia, and I were already a force to be reckoned with since we worked together on the Hit Squad.

We got out of the car and told Big Kev to wait for us with the car running. We were all checking our surroundings to make sure that Lily didn't have any bodyguards with her. I got a ping on my work phone and saw that Zontae had text me and said they had taken care of four guards that were posted around the building. He said that he had not seen anymore, and we were clear to approach. He said they would still be watching. I relayed the message to Kia and Tan, and we headed to the back of the hotel to go through the window that Arco had paid a maid to leave open.

The hotel was a small one that was less populated which I am sure was used for people having affairs. It wasn't as seedy as a pay by the hour one, but I was still shocked that someone like Lily would frequent a place like this. We got to the window, and luckily, it was big enough for Tan and me to get through. Tan went in first to check it out. From the layout that Gunner sent us, the hotel rooms were setup like apartments. With this one, the window was in the kitchenette. Tan went in and peeked his head back out to wave us in. I helped Kia in and then hefted myself up into the window.

When I got in the kitchen, I had a moment of déjà vu. A smell hit my nose and almost knocked my ass out. I looked at Tan and Kia, and they had their noses scrunched up, too. Tan took the lead and we pulled out our guns. He checked the first bedroom and shook his head no. As we got closer to the second one, there were moans coming from the room. Also, the stench of funky pussy was getting stronger. I was starting to wonder if I was cursed or some shit. Kia and Tan got on either side of the door and I took lead and eased the door open. When I saw the scene before me, I swear my ass was scarred for life.

Lily's old ass had her legs split open and some woman was eating that rotted-out, shriveled up pussy like it was her last meal. The smell was overwhelming, and I wished I had put on a mask.

Kia and Tan finally came in behind me and before I knew it, Kia had grabbed the woman by the hair and was beating her ass in the head with her gun. She had the woman's honey blonde hair wrapped around her fist and was doing damage.

Tan ran over and pulled her off while I had my gun on Lily. I finally got a look at the woman's face and threw my head back and laughed.

"Ain't this about a bitch, it's the chicken hoe! I should have known it was your funky ass. Now, I know why you smell like you do. Bitches will drink pineapple juice to make their shit smell good. Your ass off over here drinking rotten prune juice pussy!

"Fuck you! You can't talk to me like that anymore! My daddy is going to fuck you up once he finds out how you are talking to me! If he doesn't kill you, I know my man will!" Chicken Hoe yelled.

Kia broke away from Tan and punched her in the mouth. Tan went to stop it, and I waved him off. That bitch had that ass whooping coming!

I turned my attention to Ms. Prune Pussy. She was staring at me like she really hated my black ass! Oh well, the feeling was fucking mutual. I got on the phone and told Arco to bring my bag in.

"So, Lily, while we wait on some of my materials, I just want to know why you just couldn't leave the shit alone. I mean, women get cheated on all the time and don't go bat shit crazy like your ass," I said, as I looked around the room.

"Maybe because Calvin gave what was mine to that hoe! He was mine after that bitch broke him, and she should have stayed her Black ass away! Then, she had the nerve to fuck him and get pregnant with the babies that should have been mine! I woke up in the hospital and that motherfucker had given them permission to yank out my fucking uterus just so that bitch could be the only one to have his babies! I wish like hell their black ass daughter was never born. I told Doug to burn that little bitch when she was born, and his ass fucked it up! I hope that she dies in labor along with your fucking babies, and then maybe you will know my pain!" she yelled.

I swear I felt my fucking eyes twitch and grow lighter. I have never wanted to torture somebody as bad as I did this bitch! I looked around the room and started preparing for her introduction into my world. I went to the closet and found what I wanted. I had told Tan to tie both these bitches up. I was so ready to make these bitches suffer that my dick was almost standing at attention, and I had to adjust it.

I went to the part of my mind that my doctor told me to keep locked down because she was afraid of what I would do if I completely let go. But this bitch just had to open her funky ass mouth and wish death on my heart and my seeds.

I pushed the thought of my wife and seeds deep down into my lockbox of emotions and shut off everything but the craving to cause pain.

I had plugged up one of the things I needed as Arco came from the back window with my kill bag. I went in the kitchenette and got out the small tub of butter that was left in the fridge. I looked up and noticed Kia watching me. She then asked, "Viper, can you let me have Gena? I need to find out about my baby, and she is the only one that knows where Ray and my baby are? I see in your eyes that you are ready to go full out. I just need her alive long enough to give me the information. Remember, that's your niece out there, and she needs medical attention. After we get what we need, I will help you skin that bitch alive.

I nodded and walked into the other room. Lily was looking at me with hate, but she would soon be looking at me with fear. I looked over at Gena, and now the bitch was scared and fighting back tears. I pulled up a chair and brought over the iron that had heated up and had steam coming out of the bottom. I looked over at Gena because I knew that's where I would get my answers.

"So, Chicken Hoe, where is my brother?" I asked.

"I don't know. He said he was going out of town," she lied.

I grabbed the butter and scooped it out with my hands and flung it on Lily's funky ass, wrinkled pussy. I looked at Gena and said, "I don't like liars, Gena. I usually don't help people that lie to me, but since you like Ms. Prune Pussy, I figured I could at least get out some of the wrinkles for you.

I pressed the hot steam iron on Lily's buttered pussy and started ironing that shit like I was trying to get paid for it. Her skin was blistering up and she was screaming in horror as the tears came down her face. Part of her skin burned onto the iron so when I lifted it up, it looked like cheese peeling off a pizza.

Lily had passed out or had a heart attack. I would bring that bitch back in a minute. Gena was crying with tears and snot running down her face.

"Are you ready to talk now? If not, I can make sure to knock some more wrinkles out the stanky cunt for you. Then, I can iron your fucking tongue because I'm sure that motherfucker needs to be sterilized after sucking on Geritol pussy all night.

"Okay, okay. I will tell you what you want to know! Just don't hurt her anymore! Can't you see she can't take it?" Gena cried.

"Bitch, I don't give two fucks about your pussy partner. Now, answer the fucking question before you really make me go off."

She sniffled and said, "Ray, Derrick, and Doug have set up a hit to kill you all tomorrow, either during or after the funeral. I'm not sure which one because Doug and Derrick didn't trust me so they wouldn't talk in front of me. My father is Romero and he's going to be there too."

Kia walked over and said, "Where is Rylei? Has she been sick?"

Gena shook her head no and replied, "When I took her, I hired a nurse to come and sit with her in the daytime. They cleared her yesterday, and all she has to do is make her doctor's appointments."

I watched Kia let out the breath she was holding. I knew she was worried about Rylei's safety like we all were with her being born early.

"Where is Ray?" I asked.

"Ray moved us to a condo out in Paragon Mills. The address is in my phone over there. That's where Rylei is," she answered.

I looked at her because she was trying to play me. I wiped butter on Lily's cheek and set the iron on her face and pressed down. I could hear her skin sizzling as the iron burned into her flesh. The scent of it was strong in this room. Lily woke straight up as soon as the heat touched her face. Her ass wasn't talking that shit now. I was happy we got the information of where Ray was and most importantly Rylei. It was time to make these bitches suffer and get back to the house to my wife.

Tomorrow was the funeral, and I was still dealing with the emotions that losing my father brought on. I started taking my anger and pain out on Lily because this bitch set a lot of this shit in motion just because a man didn't want her. I pulled out my skinning knife and started slicing her face off piece by piece. She was crying and screaming, but I had too much on my mind to really and truly hear her. I took the knife and slit her throat after there was no more skin on her face.

Kia took over when it came to Gena. I watched as she took a scalpel and cut off Gena's eyelids and said, "Bitch, you are about to join your father in the afterlife. But, before you do, I want to send you with as much pain as possible. I mean, you like to swallow everybody's nut, so you might as well experiment with other shit, too."

Kia used the mouth gag to pry her mouth open and lock it in place. She poured the jar that had the acid in it down her throat. Bloody red foam instantly started coming out. Gena gagged and took her final breath. I got on my phone and called Zontae so he could come in and do clean up. We gathered up our stuff and climbed back out the window so we could head back to the house.

While we were riding, Tan asked, "Are you ready for tomorrow? I mean, I'm not gonna lie and say that the plan is perfect because a lot of shit can go wrong with it. We need to make sure that Anton and Corey have everything in place because this is our family we are talking about. My father is shady as hell, and I don't trust his ass. I want to just go and grab Rylei, but I know the plan has to be done first so we can leave."

I knew where he was coming from because we usually didn't let outsiders help us plan. Now, here we were placing the fate of our squad into the hands of two men that we knew very little about personally. That's another reason I brought in Zontae and Mesa to help us with it tomorrow. I trusted both of them with my life and my family's lives. We had been friends for years and in business together for the same amount of time. He made sure all my bodies stayed buried, and I made sure that he had certain coverage for his other business. But that was a story for another time.

"I feel you, Tan. Believe me. This shit is not easy for me either, but we are dealing with the mob. And until we can get some shit in place to protect all of us, we have to be cautious and use all the resources that are available. Don't worry Tan and Kia; Rylei will be back with us soon." I answered.

"I get it. Believe me. I just think something is strange about the whole situation, that's all. Uncle Corey has always been on the up and up so I trust him to watch our backs. But my father can be bought by the highest bidder, as well as pussy. I wouldn't put it past him to make a deal with the Italians and turn us in or kill us. When we get down to Cuba, we need to have the compound swept for cameras and bugs. That's the type of shit that my father would do to get any information he can use against us," Tan replied.

What Tan said had me thinking about the plan. I think I needed to move some things around just in case there was some bullshit going on. I also texted Kole and told him what I needed him to do before we touched down in Cuba. I wanted to be prepared in case things were shady when we got down there.

We finally made it back to the house and went our separate ways. I decided to take a shower in the basement in case I still had blood or body fluids on me from killing those bitches. After I finished, I went upstairs to lie up under my wife. I tried the door and it was locked up tight. I didn't have the energy to break it down, so I decided to sleep in the guest room tonight. But she would just have to get over that shit in the morning. When she signed those papers, her ass was signing up to deal with my ass for eternity, fuck life. If I went to hell so was she. That's just how much I couldn't live without her.

I sat down on the bed in the guest room and let my mind wonder about what would happen tomorrow. Everything was about to change in my life, and I was anxious to be settled. I wanted to be able to enjoy a more laid-back life, but I also wanted to continue doing missions. Once we got to Cuba, we would need to have a serious heart to heart.

I said a prayer that everything went off well tomorrow because not only would the plan be implemented, I would be saying goodbye or more like see you later to my city. All the memories of my moms and pops were here, and I was having a hard time letting go. Tomorrow, I would have to say goodbye to him for good as they lowered him into the ground. I missed him being here and that shit had me shook. My last thought before I drifted off to sleep was of my pops and I laughing at the kitchen table. A smile graced my mug as I finally went to sleep.

# Chapter 14-Kyra

I woke up with a foot in my face and saw that Aciana had climbed in the bed with us. Her head was at the foot of the bed and feet were of course on mine and her father's faces. I was so happy to have her back that I watched her sleeping in her bed for two hours last night. I eased out of the bed and headed into the bathroom to take a shower. On the door, I saw the black dress hanging up and instantly started crying.

It hit me that today was the day I officially said goodbye to my mama. I would never be able to hold her again, all because of a jealous ass bitch. If Camille wasn't already dead, I swear I would have found her trifling ass and fucked her up for taking away my heart. My mama didn't deserve that shit, and I felt so lost without her.

I cried most of the night and Ace just held me in his arms and rubbed my back. I was so thankful I had him and that he was officially my husband now. I rubbed my belly because AJ was kicking up a storm this morning. I guess he felt his mama's pain. I decided to burn a lavender candle to help me calm down because Doc still considered me high risk due to the stress and my blood pressure.

After I took care of my hygiene, I walked over the hotel closet and grabbed a maternity dress out of the suitcase. I pulled it on and went out and sat on the chaise lounge on the balcony, watching the sky change from black to a pink and orange color. I heard the patio door creak open, and I knew it was Ace.

He sat down in the chair beside me and grabbed my hand and said, "Ky, what are you doing up so early? Ma, you barely slept last night, and you and my son need y'all rest."

I smiled at my husband because he was always worried about me and his son. I responded, "Baby, I know. Your daughter is actually the one who woke me up with a kick to the face. Her little behind has to stop creeping into our bed at night because I wake up with bruises every time."

Ace started laughing and nodded his head. "Yeah, baby girl got a kick, too! She almost kicked me in the nuts last night. She would have fucked my shit up, and then she wouldn't be having her four other brothers and sisters."

My head snapped around quicker than a motherfucker.

"Aciana must have kicked your ass in the head! I am not having any more babies, Ace. We have a boy and a girl, so we good as done. Ain't another baby popping out of this coochie, so you can forget that shit!" I replied.

Ace started laughing again, but I was dead ass serious. There would be no more little ones in the Masters' household after AJ.

"Shit, that's my pussy now, and I am not pulling out, so you can forget that shit! My pull-out game is faulty. My dick gets lazy in the pussy, so his ass has to sleep in it. It's not my fault you got good pussy. My seeds have to play somewhere," Ace joked.

"Well no kitty for you then until I get on some birth control or you have to use a condom. I'm not playing, Ace," I responded.

He laughed again and answered, "Shit, I will turkey baste my nut all in you while you sleeping just so I can get more babies. Watch and see. If the Lifetime bitches can do it, so can your husband."

I laughed until my sides began to hurt. This nigga looked serious as hell when he said that shit! He bet not do shit like that for real, or I was going to beat his ass!

He stared at me and grabbed my other hand and pulled me up onto his lap. I felt his third leg poking me, and I knew our wedding night was cut short by a certain tiny person in the bed. I would have to do something special for him once the funeral was over. I would get Kia or Aja to babysit while we officially celebrated being one.

"Ky, baby, I got something I need to talk to you about. Do you remember when I said I wanted to leave Nashville?"

"Yes, you were talking about it a few days ago, and I told you that you don't have to leave here if it's for me. I will be with you no matter where you are or what profession you have," I replied.

He kissed me on the neck, and I sat back on his chest.

"I love you for saying that. It means the world to me Ky, I thought about what you said, and some opportunities came up that helped me make my decision. I met my father, Corey, the other day, and he wants me to bring my family down to Cuba to get to know him and that side of my family. He also says he has a business idea he wants to run by me. I think it would be good for us, and the best part is Ro and I found a big compound where we

222

can all live side by side. We will keep our houses in Nashville in case it doesn't work out there, or we want to come back and visit. I am letting Arco run the drug business here once we get everything back under our control. He's proved his loyalty, and it's time for him to be rewarded."

I looked at my man and was surprised that he was really giving up the day-to-day drug operations. I smiled and said, "Baby, I am so proud of you. I hope the business your father wants you to run makes you happy because you deserve it. I am excited to be moving to Cuba if even for a little while. I can't believe we all will be living there soon. That means our son will be born there. I need to find an OB doctor as soon as we land."

"No need. Doc is sending a friend of his down that will live in one of the guest houses until you and Aja deliver. Doc is coming down too to set up a free hospital here. Of course, you know one of the guest houses will have our own personal care facility. So, no need to worry, Ky. I got it all taken care of. I hate to bring this up with you actually smiling now, but it's time to get ready for the funeral. Aja picked out a hat for you and her to wear in honor of your mother since she loved her church hats," he said, pointing to a box on the couch inside.

I felt better after talking to Ace because I knew that once the funeral was over, I would be able to get away and regroup for a while. All I had to do now was try to make it through this funeral without breaking down.

## Ro/Viper

It was the day of my pops and Ms. Shelly's funeral. Kyra and I had agreed to do it all on one day so that we wouldn't go through the pain of having two funerals. We were all sleep deprived from searching for Rylei, Aciana, and taking care of our enemies along the way. We had Aciana home. Now, we just needed Rylei.

Kyra was taking her mother's death hard, and Doc was worried about her and baby Ace. He was now a permanent fixture with us until Kyra and Aja delivered.

We had security all around the funeral home where we were having the services. I couldn't take any chances with all of my family being in one place. Ray and his fuck crew had been quiet for the past week, and I had a feeling that some shit was going down soon.

I noticed that the limo we were in pulled up and we were at the funeral home. I looked over at Aja and she already had tears running down her cheeks. I grabbed my baby's hand and squeezed it. She had been my rock since I found out about Ray killing my father. Her stomach seemed to be getting bigger every day, and I hated that my baby couldn't even enjoy being pregnant with all the shit that was going on. I was worried that she was being too strong for everyone else, and I had Doc checking her blood pressure to make sure that she was okay.

Plus, she hadn't spoken to me since I tricked her into our marriage. I hoped that shit didn't backfire and make my girl leave me.

"Baby girl, are you alright? You haven't said anything since we left the safe house. You can't keep that shit bottled up or your ass will mess around and lose my seeds. Then, I would have to go to your funeral next," I joked.

She smiled and put her hand on top of mine and said, "Ro, I promise I'm fine. I just need for this

226

to all be over. I'm worried about Kyra because she's so stressed out about Ms. Shelly's death. I am just ready for all of us to get back to normal or as normal as we can be."

I watched her fidgeting with the wedding set that I had bought her and asked, "So, will you be keeping that on since I tricked you into marriage?"

She smiled a little and said, "Even though you tricked me, and I will get you back for that by the way, I am happy that you are my husband. I am just devastated about Ms. Shelly and sad that you lost your dad. I just want the two people I love so much to not have to go through this pain."

I watched as tears flowed from her eyes, and I wiped them away.

I pulled her onto my lap and held her close. She smelled like strawberries today, and it was helping to calm me down. I needed that because losing my last parent was doing something to me that I couldn't explain. I needed to see my head doctor, but I needed to find my missing niece more.

"Baby, I promise that Kyra and I will be fine. Just don't stress yourself too much, okay?" I said.

She smiled and replied, "Okay, baby. I will try not to."

We got out and went into the small funeral home and sat in the front row with the crew. Ace sat beside me, and my man looked bad. He had bags under his eyes from not sleeping, and his beard was in need of a trim. Hell, we all looked bad. I was hoping that we would all get better once this shit was all behind us. I looked over at Kyra and she was just staring at her mother's coffin and rocking. I tapped Doc and nodded in her direction. He nodded back and sat on the other side of her.

About that time, the pastor of Ms. Shelly's church went to the podium to start the services. He said a few words, and we had a member of the church sing "Amazing Grace". After she finished, it was time for the video presentation they put together for Pops and Shelly. The screen rolled down from the ceiling and Boyz II Men started playing in the background. Tears rolled down everyone's face as pictures of Pops and Ms. Shelly started playing on the screen. The tightness in my chest was unbearable, and I felt like I couldn't breathe. I missed him so much and my brother was the one that took him away from me. The screen paused on a picture of Pops. The music stopped abruptly, and I thought maybe it was a glitch in the system until I heard my pop's and mom's voices coming from the speakers.

They were arguing about her cheating and Ray not being his son. Everybody gasped in horror as they heard my mom being murdered by my own father on the tape, or should I say his other side. I was fucked up and didn't know what to think about what the fuck I just heard.

"Ro, baby talk to me what's going on in your head?" Aja asked.

I shook my head from side to side because I couldn't express how I felt without literally blowing up. The next thing I heard was the song "Celebrate Good Times" coming through the speaker and the video changed to Ray dancing and smiling. This motherfucker was behind this sick ass shit. Then, he spoke and said, "What's up, big brother? You mad, right? Well, guess what? I don't give a fuck about your feelings. I killed your crazy ass pappy, and it made my dick hard doing it, too. You see he made the mistake of killing my moms and taking shit that didn't belong to him, so his ass had to die. Simple as that Ro or Viper, hell, whatever your crazy ass is going by. You didn't have my back when I needed you the most, so we are no longer brothers. You are now the enemy and you will be treated as such, along with those two backstabbing motherfuckers, Ace and Tan.

And let's not forget my thot ass baby mama. Kia, don't worry about Rylei. She has a new mama now that is actually a real woman. Fucks me right and takes care of home. Tan can have your mannish ass! Well, I gotta run so I can be with my real family. For the ones of you that make it, I will see you soon. For those that don't well, see you in hell!" He laughed and the screen along with the lights went off.

Ace and I looked at each other and knew some shit was going down. Arco, Tan, and Big Kev walked over to us.

"Kia, Tan, and Arco take the second limo and get to the safe house and scope it out to make sure it's okay to take the girls there. Big Kev, you are driving us. I don't trust the drivers.

Before we leave, Aja and Kyra go to the back with Kia and change out of those heels in case you have to run." Once they were back with their tennis shoes and black veil pulled down over their face, it was time to leave.

We all took out our guns ready to go to war if we had to. I grabbed Aja and we all headed for the door. Arco went out first and said it was clear. We ran out and headed towards the limos. Big Kev ran ahead of us and jumped in. Ace, Kyra,

Aja, and I ran towards the back door of the limo when, all of a sudden, the limo blew up sending us flying in the air. The last thing I remember was watching the people I loved being engulfed in flames and smoke as I hurtled to the ground and darkness closed in around me.

## Chapter 15- Ray

My cousin, father, and I watched as the limo blew up with all of our enemies in it. I was finally free of those betraying bitches. I pulled off and headed to my house so we could chill and celebrate getting rid of everyone. The babysitter we had hired had Rylei, Daria, and Dajae. Over the past week, I got to know my father and cousin and could tell we had a lot in common. I hadn't heard from my wife since yesterday which was strange, but I knew she had finals coming up, and she lived in the library during those times.

We pulled up to the house and piled out and headed inside. The subdivision was new, and I asked for mine to be in the back because the two lots on either side were empty. I paid the babysitter after she said all the girls were napping, and we sat down to watch the replay of the limo explosion. Yeah, I recorded that shit just so I could rewind and watch it over and over again.

"Son, I'm proud of you. You took out most of Calvin's crew with just one bomb. Your grandfather would be happy as hell to know that you killed Rodney," Doug said, smiling.

Derrick came back from the kitchen and said, "Where is your food at, cuz? Your shit is empty as hell!"

"Yeah, my wife was supposed to bring some this morning, but I think she's still at school," I replied.

"Look, I saw a Zaxby's down the street. I'm paying if you want something," Derrick said.

My pops and I gave him our orders and he headed out. I went upstairs to check on the girls and the twins were asleep on my bed and Rylei was in her crib sucking her fingers and nodding back off. I eased my way out of the room and headed back downstairs.

I checked my phone to see when I would be notified about the deaths. I would be the sole beneficiary of Rodney's estate which was worth hundreds of millions. I was running low on funds after paying for this house and paying someone to plant the bomb that killed everybody.

I got downstairs and didn't see my pops. I figured he might have gone into the kitchen to grab a beer since that's the only thing I had in the fridge.

"Hey Pops where you at?" I asked, walking into the kitchen.

As soon as I got around the corner, I was punched hard as hell in the face, and I hit the floor. When I looked up, I saw Ro standing over me.

"Thought we were dead, didn't you, with your stupid ass! Get your bitch ass up and sit in the fucking chair!" he said, while yanking me up by my shirt.

I scrambled up to the chair where I was able to see my pops tied to a chair. Ace, Kia, and Tan were all standing in front of us with guns.

"This can't be real! I watched all of you motherfuckers die an hour ago," I yelled.

Ro punched me in the mouth so hard it knocked out two of my teeth.

"Well, dumb ass, the people you hired was actually Tan's family. If you had bothered to check the last name, you would have realized it said Morales just like his. Luckily, he knew some people that do the explosions for the movies and shit, and they set up the bomb just to make you and some other people believe that we were either dead or injured. We switched out Aja and Kyra for body doubles because they are pregnant, and we didn't want to take the chance. Shit, I might try my hand at being a stunt double," Ro said, jokingly.

"Man, fuck you! I know I'm about to die so you can save that story telling shit and just get it the fuck over with 'cause I'm not begging you for shit!" I yelled.

Ro laughed, and Kia joined in and said, "To think I used to be in love with your stupid ass. You left me for a gold digging skank that was fucking and sucking anything that had juice in it. That bitch played you, and you fell for that shit!"

"Bitch fuck you! At least my wife ain't like your mannish, hoe ass! You bet not have touched her, or I swear I will kill your ass!" I yelled, mean mugging Kia until Tan punched me in the stomach.

"Don't disrespect her, or I swear I will break every bone in your fucking body!" Tan growled.

Aja came in and she was holding Rylei and gave her to Kia who kissed all over her face. She said, "Arco has the twins, and he's driving up to the mountains now to take them to Tyesha. Kyra, Aciana, and I are going to walk around the cul de sac since no one lives back here. That should give you some time to take out the trash. Don't worry,

237

Zontae and Mesa are out in the van and said they would watch out for us."

"Aja Lanae Casey, stay the fuck away from Zontae! Don't make me fuck you up!" Ro said.

She waved him off and left.

"Is the tape you had played true? Is that why you killed the only father who ever loved you with your ungrateful ass?" he asked.

"Man, fuck his crazy ass! He killed our fucking mama and you standing here mad at me! His ass changed into a monster and killed her like she was nothing to him! I would pull the trigger time and time again if I could. Your ass just blind to it because you are just as crazy as he was, and you will probably kill that bitch that just left because it's in your DNA."

"So, since it's kill a pappy day, Tan take care of Doug," Ro said, as Tan stabbed my Pops in the throat and his body slid down out of the chair and onto the floor.

"I swear, I hate your ass! I can't wait for Lily and Camille to kill your ass. It would save the world a lot of trouble when your psychotic ass snaps," I yelled.

Kia handed my daughter over to Tan. He started kissing on her and calling her daddy's princess. I wanted to kill him where he stood, but I knew my time was up.

"Well, here's the thing, Ray. You might hate me, but I don't hate you. I have always looked out for you and loved you because you were my baby brother and that shit meant something to me. I guess we are different because it never meant shit to you. Have you heard of Sunnydale Hospital, Tan?" Ro asked.

"Hell yeah, That's that hospital that keeps getting the low rankings, but no one can shut them down because some rich ass judge owns it. I heard the roaches crawl all over the patients and that the nurses let you stay shitty for days. It's a real hell hole. I even heard the male orderlies fuck the patients, male and female patients," Tan replied.

"Well, little brother, I might not have the heart to kill you, but I damn sure am going to make you suffer for turning your back on us. By the way Kia, show him the video."

Kia took out her phone and played a video. My heart broke into a million pieces as I watched my wife eating Lily's pussy. It switched to her tied to a chair confessing that she was going to kill me and take my money along with her father Romero. I felt like a fucking fool for being played by that bitch! I watched as Kia beat and tortured her before finally killing her. Even though she conned me, I cried while the life left her beautiful body. Kia put the phone up and grabbed her hunting knife from its sheath on her hip.

"Bro, I tried to warn you, but you wouldn't listen. Now, you have to pay the price. I will make sure that money is always there for your care. I mean, Sunnydale can't be that bad, right?" Ro said, and turned around and left the kitchen.

Tan came and kissed Kia on the lips and left with my baby girl. My heart hurt knowing this would be the last time I would ever see her. I looked up into Kia's beautiful face, and for the first time, I had regrets for all the shit I had done to her and my brother. I wished I could go back and change the decisions that I had made, but judging by the look on her face, it was too late.

"Kia, I'm sorry. Just make sure that Rylei knows something good about me. I got caught up, ma. I was in a messed up space. Just tell her that I loved her and loved her mama very much."

Kia stared into my eyes and gave me a hug and kissed my neck. She straddled me and pulled me closer. My dick bricked up just from this brief touch. I felt an excruciating pain in my neck and then I felt absolutely nothing. I couldn't move at all and Kia was holding me up. I saw her pull something from behind her back and it was her hunting knife.

"I used to love you with everything in me, but you killed that love and there is no fucking forgiveness just revenge. I just severed your spine, so you are paralyzed. I figured you wouldn't need it anyway with your spineless ass! Oh, I paid off the nurses and orderlies at the home. You will be the shittiest, nastiest, patient they will have. Big Bubba is going to have so much fun with you. He likes fresh tight assholes, just like you. I might stop by to make sure that you are suffering. Rylei will never know you even existed. She already has a father. Bye, Ray. I hope you suffer every hour, minute, and second of the rest of your miserable ass life," she said, as she left the room and I blacked out.

## Chapter 16-Aja

I was smiling from ear to ear as we made our way from the plane into the awaiting SUVs. We were headed to the compound that would be our new home for however long we wanted it to be. All our enemies were dead, and it was time to start living again. I held my husband's hand and looked into his eyes. Ro was my everything and he had saved me from a life of fear and pain. I wasn't happy about the way we got married, but I was happy at the fact that we were married. Ro had all of us dress up so we could arrive in style he said. I was wearing a red, off the shoulder dress that flowed down my body and touched the tops of my feet. As a matter of fact, Kia had on a blue one, and Kyra had on a yellow one. My hair was flowing down my back and pinned to one side of my head with a big red rose. My baby was in a white, linen pants suit with a red undershirt. He had a red rose attached to his jacket.

We pulled up to the compound, and I had never seen anything like it. There was a guard's station and the guard waved us through after checking with the driver. Each house was huge and had its own entrance. Ro said that behind the houses was a courtyard where each house could go out the back door and have access. We all headed toward the courtyard and it was so beautiful. I knew I would be spending a lot of time out here. Flowers were everywhere and there was a huge fountain in the middle. Coming out of the big, white house was my mother and my father on a cane. I ran over to them and hugged them both.

"I am so glad you are walking, Dad. You look so much better than the last time I saw you. Hi, Mama. You look so pretty," I said.

I had talked to them both every day for the past few weeks, getting to know them. While they were in the mountains, they got married because my father said he couldn't live without her anymore. I was so happy for them, and I was excited that they were here so we could deepen the bond.

"Quick hogging our parents, Aja!" Kia said.

They both told Ace and Kia that they were to call them Mom and Dad also. They knew how April treated us and wanted to show us three what a parents' love was really about.

"Well, let's get this show on the road," Calvin said.

I was confused as to what they were talking about until everyone went around the corner to another part of the courtyard. It had a heart shaped flower arch and a red rose, petal aisle. At the end of the aisle was my husband, standing there looking fine as hell! My father grabbed my hand and my mom grabbed my other hand. We walked down the aisle as one, and it meant everything. April might have made my childhood hell, but she didn't take my future. That was standing in front of me with a smile on his face. My father and mother both gave me a kiss on the cheek and gave me away to this handsome man.

The minister welcomed everyone, and I didn't hear a word. I was too busy staring into Ro's eyes and falling in love all over again. He held both of my hands and was rubbing circles around my palms.

"Excuse me, I was telling you two to say your vows," the minister said.

I looked back at Ro, and he looked at me. We both said at the same time, "Our love beats all!"

## Epilogue- 4 months later

**Aja**

I was in the nursery, standing over my babies' cribs. Two months ago, I was blessed with three of the most handsome sons you could ever ask for. I went into labor fast, and they were delivered within an hour. Viper likes to take credit for that since we were in the middle of fucking in the courtyard when my water broke. I was so exhausted afterwards that when they came around with the birth certificates, I just signed. I was still pissed off to this day about their names, but I didn't feel like arguing with him about it. All three were the spitting image of their father and he was on cloud nine, spoiling them.

I felt arms wrap around me, and I knew it was my man.

"You are supposed to be resting, Mrs. Casey. You have been up with the boys all night. You need to sleep while they sleep," Viper said, kissing my neck.

"I am. I just wanted to check in one more time to make sure they didn't need anything. You know I hardly get my hands on them between my mom and dad and their aunts and uncles. And let's not forget their spoiling ass daddies," I said.

Viper laughed and picked me up bridal style. He carried me across the hall to our bedroom, and laid me down on the bed, and kissed me. I started to deepen it when he said, "Baby girl, I wish I could beat that pussy up right now, but the big meeting is in a few minutes. You get some rest and wait on daddy to come home."

He kissed me and left. So much had changed, and I was happier than I had ever been. Ace, Kole, and Ro now ran two businesses. One was a nightclub Ace's dad gave him in the downtown tourist area that was doing well, and also, Ro took over The Hit Squad, doing his father's position, which was training and setting up missions. He hired one of the best planners to help him plan them. Yep, you guessed it, me! Vixen can never fully retire. She has too much to do. Kyra and I had opened an online spa product boutique and we were working on it while we took care of our boys. My mom and dad lived next door and were the absolute best! Tyesha was still in the states recuperating from all the damage Romero did to her. She was still being cautious because Derrick was still out there and no one could find him. We were slowly building our bond as sisters, and I could tell she was changing. I could tell that a certain Tech Specialist had something to do with that change. Every time I bring it up, she says they are just friends. Yeah, right! I will let Annitia tell you that story! Life was good, and I couldn't wait to see what was in store for us.

## Viper

A brother was on top of the world, and I couldn't help but be excited. I had my family, my friends, and my career. I had been going on a regular basis to see my head doctor when I flew into the states to do business. I was taking my meds but shit, let's face it, my crazy ass always going to flip out. I was sitting, thinking about my wife and how I could talk her into having another baby. I needed a little girl that looked just like her. Hell, she would be well guarded with her cousin Ace Junior, and her brothers, Cannon, Colt, and Caliber. Yeah, fuck y'all! Those are my sons' names, and if you don't like that shit, we can talk about it over a plate of chicken and some tea!

## Ace & Kyra

Well, it looks like Aja has already told all of our business. We were doing well and spoiling our daughter, Aciana, and our new son, Ace Junior or

AJ. We loved the island life and so was Aciana. The extended family we had met has been great, and it has been nice to just be normal. Ace's father had moved closer to us so he could spend time with his grandkids. The only thing we worried about now was how to spend our day.

## Kia

I had been laying low so I could spend my time with my baby girl and bae. His mom, Amelia, had moved in with us, and she was helping out with Rylei. My baby girl was so amazing, I couldn't even explain it with words. Tan and I were still going strong. He was still doing missions with the Hit Squad, and I would be joining him soon. We had a few hiccups; the main one being his ex-wife moving onto the compound next door to us. She was hateful as hell, and I wanted to slice her face off.

Their daughter Tanna was my baby though. She was five going on fifteen, but I loved her feisty self. Tan kept saying that Sasha being here was temporary, but I had a feeling her ass was up to something.

The second hiccup was that Tan wanted to get married, and I wasn't ready. My heart had been stomped on, and I wasn't completely healed yet. I was hoping that he would understand, but every chance he got he was bringing it up.

Ray was still at Sunnyvale being neglected. Enough said about that fuck boy!

I was on my way to the meeting that we were supposed to have with Anton about the terms they set not to retaliate against us. It had been put off with all the babies being born and funerals. Anton told me to come ten minutes earlier because he had something to talk to me about in private. When I got there, he was sitting at his desk eye fucking me.

That shit wasn't anything new since we touched down in Cuba.

"You wanted to see me, Anton?" I asked, ready to get this shit over.

He licked his lips and his eyes roamed my body again. He finally said,

"The Italians came to me and they want you to do three missions for them. They have heard good things about the Reaper and they want to use her services to get rid of their top targets that have proven to be hard to kill."

I nodded my head because it didn't bother me at all. It was what I did for a living, and I was the baddest bitch in the game for hits. It would just be someone else paying this time. I got up to leave and he stopped me.

"Kia, there is one more item of business that we need to attend to before you leave. Please have a seat while I explain," Anton said.

I sat down and waited for him to tell me what he wanted. I couldn't wait to get to the conference room and get away from his creepy ass. Then he opened his mouth and said, "Let me get straight to the point. Your family is indebted to me for saving you from the Italians. That means that if I make one call and pull my support, your whole family will be targets, even those precious babies."

I looked at this motherfucker like he had lost his mind for threatening my family. I wanted to take the blade out of my pocket and slice his throat, but there was too much security around.

"What do you want, Anton?" I replied.

He laughed and licked his nasty ass lips again and said, "That's easy. I want you to be my wife."

**The End for Aja and Ro but the beginning for others...**

**Find out what happens with Akia, Tan, Gunner, Tyesha, and Kole in: D-City Hit Squad**

## Bonus: Find out what happened to April below.

## April

After being picked up that night after fleeing Aja's house, I thought everything was going to be alright. I was dead wrong! A man named Tyler picked me up that night, and he had been beating me black and blue ever since. That was four months ago. I was currently walking down Dickerson Road trying to get up the two hundred dollars that I needed to give Tyler in order to not get beat.

I used to get paid thousands to fuck men, and now I get paid ten dollars to suck dick and twenty to be fucked. My pussy didn't even get wet anymore. A van pulled up and this tall, fine, young stallion called me over. I smiled but didn't open my mouth because four of my teeth were missing. When I got to the van, he waved me in and I got in the passenger's seat. He pulled off and we were on our way.

"So, what do you want, handsome? You can fuck me in any hole you want as long as you have the cash," I asked.

He laughed and said, "Just sit back and relax, beautiful. I have a special treat for you if you just relax," he said, handing me a red pill.

I popped the pill because I needed to get high with the way my life was going. I instantly felt myself get lighter, and I wanted to ask him what this was because it was the shit! I tried to stay awake, but it was no use. The pill had knocked me out. When I came to, I was hanging upside down over a metal tub. I looked around and saw other bodies hanging upside down with tubes in their bodies and blood running through them into the tubs.

I heard voices talking and closed my eyes and pretended to be asleep.

"Zontae, we have five shipments going out tonight, and we need more B positive and AB positive. Do you want the B positive mixed?" the voice sounded like the same guy that picked me up.

A deeper voice answered, "Yeah, mix it with the Molly and put B Molly on it. The young V-set will go crazy for that shit and pay anything. I see you finally caught that bitch! You might as well open your eyes, April. I know you are awake."

I opened my eyes and a handsome man with sunglasses on was looking back at me. There was something different about him that scared me and excited me at the same time.

"If you wanted a threesome all you had to do was ask," I said, trying to talk my way out of my current situation.

"Bitch, nobody wants none of your used up, dry ass, fish market ass pussy!" the younger one said.

They both laughed and the one with the sunglasses said, "Viper wanted you to know he warned you in the kitchen that you would meet the devil if you ever crossed him."

I immediately started crying because Viper whispered in my ear in the kitchen that I would die by the hands of a devil if I crossed him. I guess I shouldn't have taken that money. I looked at him and asked, "Are you the devil?"

He smiled and took off his glasses, and I pissed on myself! His eyes were a mixture of red and green swirls and his teeth had turned to fangs.

"No, I'm not the devil. I'm something ten times worse!"

**The end for April but the beginning if you want to check out Zontae and Mesa in my new Urban Supernatural, two-part series: D-City Underworld: Zontae's Reign, coming soon.**

Coming soon from Annitia
L. Jackson

## "An Urban Christmas Story: Ebb and Bobbi"

### Synopsis:

Ebbson (Ebb) Scribbs is one of the coldest hearted men in Nashville. He is one of the top accountants in the state and has accounts with top businesses and criminals. He loves money and money is the only thing on his mind. Life has taught him not to care about anything or anyone until something changes his cold heart.

Bobbi Cramer is a single mother, working hard to take care of her daughter, Timea. She has worked as Ebb's assistant for over a year, and puts up with his standoffish ways. Bobbi doesn't care because all she needs is a paycheck to support her child since her daughter's father is a deadbeat.

Tragedy strikes and brings the two together in unexpected ways, even as a silent enemy lurks.

Carson Mills is a married detective with a lot of secrets. He has been trying to take down the heads of D-City for years and feels that Ebb is his way to do that. He will do anything to get Ebb to rat on his clients.

Will Bobbi and Ebb live happily ever after for Christmas?

## "The Trinity Girl Chronicles: The Christmas Emerald"

### Synopsis:

The Trinity Girl Warrior's, Eliana, Jame`, and Kalyn were shocked to learn about their destiny. Now, they are determined to protect humans and angels at all costs. They have been training hard and are ready for their first mission, or are they?

The Chaos Squad has a few tricks up their sleeves as they enroll in the same school as the girls. Chaos has the perfect plan to ruin one of the human's most favorite times of the year, Christmas!

Will the Trinity Girls be able to stop them? Or will they ruin Christmas forever?

Follow the girls and their friends as they go on their first mission to save Christmas.

### "Loving a Heartless Queen"
### Synopsis:

Valentine Miller's heart didn't live up to her name. She was burned by love and had made a career out of destroying others' relationships. She is a media queen (known as the Queen of Mean) that hosts a show that exposes cheaters to their significant others. She has made a lot of enemies, and now, one of them wants her dead. In steps Arkell (Ark) Watson, a former savage turned legit. After watching the woman that he loved die because of his profession, he decides to run a security service that becomes one of the best in the country. After a run in with Valentine and subsequently saving her life, Ark starts to see another side of Valentine that makes him want to tear down the walls that she has built around her heart. As their bond grows stronger, so does the enemy's lust for revenge. Can Ark save Valentine? Not only from her would be killer, but from herself? Ever Moore, Valentine's best friend was the opposite. Everything is going well in her life, a thriving practice and new love, until something starts happening to her patients. As she starts to investigate, she uncovers a lot more than she bargained for. Will she be able to save her patients? Or will saving their lives mean giving up hers?

## About The Author:

 I would like to personally thank you for reading my first book series, D-City Chronicles. It has been an amazing experience writing about these different and complex characters. In the book, the characters deal with many issues such as mental illness, rape, and abuse. These are topics that we sometimes brush under the rug in the African American community. If you are experiencing or know someone experiencing any of these problems, please seek help.

This is book four for me, and I'm excited to be able to share my work and creativity with all of my old and new readers. As a new author in this literary world, I'm encouraged by your reviews and your willingness to read and hopefully enjoy my work.

To my publisher, Treasure Malian, I am thankful for the opportunity and humbled that you allow me to use my pen to display my craft. Treasure, you are an inspiration, and I thank you for allowing me to create books and genre hop. You allow me to think outside the box and encourage me to be creative. To my TP pen sisters, thank you for your undying love and support as I navigate as one of the newest TP Gems. Tomeika and Ty, my pen twins, thank you so much for keeping me focused and for giving me a listening ear when I need it. You two are a prayer answered to a new author. You both have helped me grow in so many ways that I don't even have room to write it. Thank you for pushing me and uplifting me. You two ladies are such a blessing, and I love you both!

To my readers... words cannot express what you mean to me. Thank you for reading my work and giving me critiques to help me better my craft.

I am always available to hear your comments and opinions. I love you, ALJ readers!!!!

**Please check out my other titles listed on Amazon and Barnes & Noble:**

D-City Chronicles Book One: Aja and Ro

D-CITY Chronicles Book Two: Aja and Ro

D-CITY Chronicles Book Three: Aja and Ro

The Trinity Girl Chronicles Book One: The Awakening

# HAVE YOU READ
# THIS?

Be sure to LIKE our Major Key Publishing

page on Facebook!

CPSIA information can be obtained
at www.ICGtesting.com
Printed in the USA
LVHW05s1945200618
581394LV00021B/365/P

9 781985 264946